I'm Not Famous, But I Use To Be!!!

Gary O. Moore

June 08

I'm Not Famous, But I Use To Be!!!

Gary O. Moore

2007

I'm Not Famous, But I Use To Be!!!

CHAPTER I

This is a story about a man who has the American dream, but wants more. His name is Roland Booker. He has a wife named Paula, who has been with him through thick and thin for 4 years now. He also has a 2-year-old son. Oh yeah, did I mention that he's in the United States military? That's right, a GI. He's been a member for five long years. All in all, he has everything he needs and wants for the time being, and this is his story through his eyes and in his words:

Every other month I go to pay our car insurance bill. What I didn't know was that this day was going to change the rest of my life. My story begins with me going into City-Wide Insurance Company. While I'm there waiting for my turn to pay, I notice Janet, our insurance agent, giving me the eye. Could I be imagining this? I looked up from the magazine that I picked up to read, just to see her smiling at me. This was really happening. What should I do? Well, let me tell you what I did. I told myself that when I pay my bill, if she makes a pass at me, I would see how far it would go. This isn't one of your typical insurance agents. Janet Peterson was very attractive, high classed, and she carried herself in a way that you knew you had to have yourself together if you were to try to take her out.

Then it was my turn to pay, and I sat before her.

"Hello Mr. Booker, or may I call you Roland?" she says.

"You can call me whatever you want, as long as you let me know when you are going to call me so I will know to answer," I say, trying to keep cool.

I felt kind of stupid saying that because she laughed at me. So I laughed along with her and handed her my check for the bill. She started asking me about my family and how the military was treating me. She was acting like she was my psychologist, as if I had one. Then she asked me about her joining the military.

"You seem to be a successful insurance agent with your own branch and all," I said. "Why would you want to give all this up for the military"?

She laughed at me again.

"I don't want to quit my job and join full time, silly. I was thinking of joining the reserve, so that I would be able to say that I've served my country."

We talked for a while until she noticed that people were getting restless.

"You better go now before I start losing customers," Janet said. "Can I call you sometime? I mean to talk about the military and all?"

After she told me that, I knew my life was taking a turn, but I didn't know in what way. So I did what any man with an ego problem in that position would do. I gave her my cell phone number and then I left.

The next day while at work my cell phone rings. I looked at the number and didn't recognize it. Then it dawned on me that it was Janet. My heart skipped a beat. I stood there for a moment and said to myself, what the heck. So I answered it. To my surprise she asked me out to lunch with her. I accepted and we agreed to meet at a Chinese buffet at noon. I was kind of nervous about what was going to take place at noontime, but to no avail I showed up like the man I was trying to be.

We sat across from each other in the small booth. I tried looking only at my food, but she saw right through me.

"What's the matter Roland? Are you nervous," she said. "Not at all Janet," I replied.

Who was I fooling? I had to loosen up some. So I started with the compliments of her beauty and the aroma of her sweet smelling perfume. After that we chatted away, getting to know each other on a more personal level. Time passed by and it was time to go back to work. So we parted, but not without her inviting me over that evening for dinner at her place.

Later that day after work I was finding myself singing to myself and having fun with my son. My wife told me I was in a good mood. I had to keep cool so she wouldn't suspect anything. She was looking kind of tense so I told her to go take a long bubble bath and relax while I take our son out for a little while. She was so excited. She gave my son and me a kiss and ran upstairs to get started. Twenty minutes later my son and I were ringing the doorbell of my soon to be mistress.

CHAPTER 2

The door opens and a sweet smelling fragrance whooshes by us. Janet is standing there with a magenta silk evening gown on. She then sees my son standing next to me. She picks him up and kisses him.

"Come on in Roland," she says. "What is this little cute boy's name?"

I told her his name and sat down in her living room. I can't help but look around, and that's because this lady had some really nice things in her house. I had to compliment her on the things she had. She told me that they were antiques that she collected over time. She was in her mid-twenties. For her to have all these nice things was amazing to me. Shortly after taking a tour of her condo she sat me down at the dining room table. My son had fallen asleep on the couch, so we didn't wake him. She had prepared an Italian dinner and it was the best Italian food I had ever eaten. After dinner we spoke about numerous things. Then she asked me if I had ever had an affair before. Of course the answer was no.

"So this will be your first time?" she said in a sweet, mellow voice as she smiled at me.

"Yes," I replied. "But why me?"

I told her that I knew she has a lot of men drooling over her everyday.

"A beautiful and successful woman like you surely has to have a special man in her life," I said.

I was shocked by her response. She told me that she does have a man but things aren't looking too good for them right now and that from the first day she saw me she wanted me at any cost.

"May I be your mistress for a while," she asked? I couldn't believe how straightforward she was about the whole situation.

"Does this answer your question?" I said as I leaned toward her and gave her a soft kiss on the lips.

That was the beginning of the end. Only I didn't know it then.

"I got to go now. It's getting late," I said.

"Don't be surprised if you fall in love with me and leave your wife," she said smiling.

"We'll see what happens," I told her.

Then I picked my son up and told her to call me when she is free.

"Are you always going to have your son with you when you are with me?" she asked?

"No, not all the time," I said.

She kissed me on the cheek and I left.

A few days had gone by and the shock of what happened the other day had worn off. Then I got a call from Janet and she wanted me to come up to her office at 6pm. Of course I go, because I haven't seen or heard from her in a few days. When I get there, she locks the door behind me and pulls down all the shades.

"What's going on," I asked her?

"I've been thinking about you for the last couple of days, and you know what? It's time to make this relationship official," she said as she smirked.

I'm looking around the office. I know the place is closed, but I'm worrying about her boyfriend popping up.

After I saw her pull up her skirt, and noticed she wasn't wearing any under garment, I said what the heck. She then lies down on her desk with her legs hanging down over the edge. This was the perfect position to show her a lot of attention.

"I haven't had a real orgasm in years, Roland. Would you like to do the honors?" she said.

I slowly take off my shirt.

I'm still in disbelief, but I follow through because my hormones took over. Everything was set as if it had been rehearsed. The sun was setting, City-Wide Insurance was closed and I have been wanting this to happen ever since I first laid eyes on Janet Peterson, my insurance agent. After months of just coming in here, paying my bill and leaving wishing I could have one night with her. Here's my chance to make my fantasy a reality. The things we did in there I had only seen in porno flicks, but now it was happening to me.

The After math:

We are both naked and chilled with sweat. As we lay cuddled on her couch in the break room, she tells me that my loving was incredible. I gave her props also. She gets up and swings my legs around. Now I'm sitting up on the couch. Man, she drained me. All I was thinking about was getting some sleep, until she got between my legs and looked up in my eyes.

"I'm house sitting for a friend of mine this weekend," she said. "I would really love for you to spend as much time with me as you possibly can. So what's your answer?"

I took a moment to think about it. I knew I was going to say yes, but I didn't want to seem too hasty. To help me answer to her liking, she goes down on me and performs some outstanding oral sex.

A couple of days go by. It's Thursday afternoon. Janet asked me to meet her at a grocery store across the street from her job. I drove around the parking lot until I saw her sitting in her car waiting for me. I pull up beside her and park my car. Before I get out, a car comes speeding up, and screeches to a halt blocking Janet and my car from leaving. Out jumps this big, angry man.

"Get over here, Janet," the man yells.

Janet looks at me and tells me to get in her car. I couldn't show my fear in front of her, and besides it wasn't like that was my wife getting out of the car. So I smoothly got out of my car, locked it and got into hers. Once I was in her car she told me that she had broken up with her boyfriend the other day and he still didn't know why. I told her that she should go out there and handle her business. She got out and told me she would be right back. There was a lot of yelling going on outside the car, and all I could think to myself was, what am I doing here and is this really worth losing everything that I have?

Just when I make up my mind to get out and go home, Janet jumps back in the car.

"I'm glad that's over with," she said.

"Is everything OK?" I asked.

Janet kissed me on the lips and tells me yes. Her ex-boyfriend was just shocked that she was seeing someone else so fast, but he didn't have any hard feelings. Yeah right! I didn't believe one word of what she just told me, especially since didn't know that I saw her give him a hug and kiss before she got back in the car. It didn't matter anyway. I was just having some fun with her. It's not like I'm married to her. So I left with her.

I asked her where she was taking me. She told me that she was taking me to the house where we are going to be this weekend so I would know how to get there.

"Don't worry, Roland," she said to me. "My boyfriend, I mean my ex-boyfriend, doesn't know where this house is."

After we go by the house, we go back to the grocery store and she kissed me good-bye.

"I have a special weekend planned for us, Roland. Just you wait and see," she said.

And with that she drove off.

CHAPTER 3

I get in my car one happy man. When I get home my wife is on the phone. I kiss her on the cheek and go upstairs. After my wife gets off of the phone she comes upstairs also. When I look at her cheek I see lipstick. Oh no. What am I going to do? Before I could come up with a plan she goes in the bathroom. Ten minutes go by and then she comes out with the lipstick no longer on her cheek. I remember thinking to myself that this is it. My heart was beating in my throat. I got in the bed pretending to be very tired. Is she going to say something to me? If not, I was not going to say anything to her. To my surprise, she got in the bed, gave me a kiss, said goodnight, and went to sleep.

The next two days go by smoothly and I figure that I'm in the clear. I treated my family extra special. We had family night on Friday. Now that it's Saturday, I tell my wife that I'm going to hang with the guys. I see the hesitation in my wife eyes, but she gives me her consent.

I kissed my son, hugged my wife, and then I left for my mistress. While I was driving my cell phone rings. I look at the screen and don't recognize the number. I didn't want to answer it in case it was Janet. I pulled over and used a payphone. When I called the number that was on my phone, it was indeed Janet. She wanted me to pick up a movie. Blockbusters was on the way, so I stopped to pick up a movie and then I was on my way again. Shortly after that I pulled up in the driveway. I got out of the car and rang the doorbell. The doorbell had a unique chime to it, nothing I ever heard before.

Janet opens the door. She is looking stunning. All she has on is a thong and a see through evening gown, and it's only three in the afternoon. I rush up to her, kissing her on the neck. Then she kicks the door shut, backs me into it and then sticks her tongue down my throat. This was going to be a good day. After a few minutes of passionate kissing, she pulls away and decides to show me around the house.

This house was amazing. Whoever owned this house had to be rich or pretty close to it! There was an Ivory grand piano in one room, the top of the line computer in another, sculptures that had to be worth thousands, and artwork on all the walls that you would only see in a museum. All the furniture was of soft white Italian leather. In the garage there was a Lamborghini with leather and wooden interior. There was also a Jaguar next to it, but I had never seen a Lamborghini that close before. Janet let me get inside the car. That Lamborghini had a 10-speaker Bose system that was all digitized and it was voice activated. I must have stayed in that car for fifteen minute playing around with all the gadgets. Janet and I then got on the computer to surf the net. We took turns on the keyboard to see who could find the nastiest porn pictures. Janet let me play on the computer while she started dinner. I couldn't resist the grand piano. I'm a piano player. I've played classical jazz piano for years. So I decided to play her some songs. I played and sang to Janet almost every song I knew. She was impressed with my singing, along with my piano play.

Time seemed to fly by, because now it was time to eat dinner. When I got to the dinner table, there before me was a six course meal with candles lit. All the lights were off. Janet wanted me to put some music on for us to listen to while we ate, and I obliged. Dinner was delicious and I was stuffed. We decided to walk off the food we just ate. Janet put on a jogging suit and we walked around the block, which was so big it took us 45 minutes.

Once we got back to the house, we stripped down and got in the Jacuzzi that was in one of the rooms in the house. There we made love. It carried on from there to the living room with a nice fireplace. Of course we had to start the fire ourselves. I started it, while Janet put the movie that I got from Blockbusters in the DVD player.

During the movie we couldn't stop fondling and kissing each other. I went old-school on her by renting the movie 9 1/2 Weeks. That movie made us both hot. After the movie Janet took me upstairs to one of the bedrooms where we had some X-rated sex. It seemed like the more we had sex, the better it got. We both dozed off for some much-needed rest. I don't know how long it was, but something made me jump up thinking it was the next day. It was the next day. It was 9 a.m. Janet was still sleep. I started talking in a panic.

"Wake up Janet! It's nine in the morning! I got to go home," I said.

Janet rolled over and told me that I didn't ever have to go home again if I didn't want to. She was either talking in her sleep or going crazy. Whatever it was, I gave her a kiss and told her to give me a day or two to let this blow over with my wife. Then I took off like a rocket.

I get home and my wife is in the kitchen making my son some breakfast. I try to give her a kiss, but she's not having it. I really did it this time, my stupid self.

"I know you are cheating on me," my wife says. "I don't know with whom and I can't prove it for sure but when I can, you my friend are history. I swear if you are cheating on me, your son and I are going home to my parents and you will hear from a lawyer."

What could I say.

"You know I love you girl. Stop saying all that madness."

Man, am I scared now. I try to play like everything is cool by playing with my son until it's time for him to eat. Then I go upstairs to get some more sleep. Before I go upstairs I tell my wife to wake me up at 3:00pm so I can catch the football game on TV.

CHAPTER 4

A couple of weeks go by and everything is back to normal in the Booker household. In those couple of weeks I haven't seen or heard from Janet. One day my cell phone rings while I'm out at the basketball court. It was Janet. I asked her what was going on because I said a couple of days, and she hadn't called me for a couple of weeks. She cleared her throat and told me that somebody broke into the house she was house sitting. I almost died. I couldn't believe it. Somebody stole paintings and sculptors and even the Lamborghini stereo system.

"Do the police have any leads?" I asked.

Janet told me that there were unfamiliar fingerprints throughout the house. The police asked her if she had any visitors while she was there. That bitch said no. Man, I broke out in a cold sweat.

"Why did you say that," I said? "I was all over that house. Some of those fingerprints are mine."

"I didn't want you to get into trouble, seeing that you are married. I told them that the fingerprints could be my boyfriends," Janet said.

I wanted to hang up on her.

"Wait a minute. You just said that you told them that you didn't have any company," I said puzzled.

"Roland, I'm scared for you. I didn't even realize I said that to them. It didn't work anyway. The fingerprints didn't match his. What should I do?" she asked.

I told her she better go down to the precinct and tell the truth. Now the regrets are overwhelming me. I'm feeling lightheaded.

"I'll call you later," Janet says. Then she hung up the phone.

The rest of the day I'm feeling sick to my stomach. When I get home my wife thinks that I got hurt playing basketball. If she only knew what was going on. I told her that I was going to bed to try to sleep it off. Who was I fooling? I must have laid there in bed for hours before I dozed off.

The next day still feeling sick at work, two detectives come in to take me down to the precinct for questioning. I don't even fight them. I told my supervisor that I was taking an early lunch and I left with them.

Down at the police station I tell them the whole story about Janet and I, without the details of intimacy of course. I'm thinking that would be enough for me to clear myself. It wasn't like I was guilty anyway. One of the investigating officers said that I told them a pretty good story, but I was full of shit.

"What do you mean?" I asked them. "Didn't Janet Peterson from City-Wide Insurance Company talk to you all yesterday?"

"No!" they both say to me in unison. Then one of them says that they got a witness who gave them my license plate number off of my car.

"If what you were telling us is true, why would she lie to us in her statement?" they asked.

I had to explain to them that she was trying to hide our affair. I hate being around cops and hate even worse being locked up. They gave me one chance before they locked me up, and that was to contact Janet to verify my story. Just my luck they couldn't find Janet anywhere.

They told me that I could either post bail or wait until they caught up with Janet. I used my one call to call my supervisor. I didn't trust anybody else. My supervisor was pretty cool. I knew he would get me out and not tell my wife about this ordeal. After explaining to him briefly what was up, he said he'd be right down.

I let him know that as soon as I get out I would pay him back for the bail money. Thirty minutes later the guard was letting me out. I was walking around the corner and saw my supervisor. Before I could thank him, my wife stepped out from behind him. My heart froze mid beat.

"Hey honey," I said surprisingly to her. "We have got to talk."

My supervisor told me that we—meaning him, our commander, and me—were going to have a meeting about this situation in the morning. I used to think he was cool, but now I see. My wife had posted bail for me, and all my supervisor had to say to me was that he would see me first thing on the morning.

On the way home I knew that I had to explain. I had to tell her the truth. I had to be a man. I spilled my guts. Told her everything. She was quiet for a moment, and then she blew up, just as I expected. I still hear her voice like it was yesterday.

"How could you do this to me and your son? We are over. I knew you were having an affair. I tried to tell myself it wasn't so, but now that it's in the open I have no choice but to leave you," she told me.

Oh man, I tried not to cry, but I couldn't hold back the tears. That was it, the end of all that I held dear to my heart. My family is gone, but before I try to get them back, I have to get out of this situation with the law. Then it dawned on me that the military might get me as well. That was the last night I would spend with my family.

The next day I took them to the airport. As hard as it was for me, I had to keep a straight face when I told my son that I would see him soon. All I could say to my wife was I'm sorry. I promised her that I would make it up to her some day. I stayed at the airport until their plane took off and that was that.

As soon as I left the airport I had to report to my commander. I got there just in time for our meeting. I went in and sat down. I'm looking at my supervisor still mad at the fact that he told on me. None of this would be happening if he had kept his mouth shut. My commander tells me that they are going to court-martial me for committing adultery.

"How are you all going to find me guilty of that charge?" I said as I smiled.

Then he asked me if I knew a Miss Janet Peterson. The commander had a signed and notarized signature from Janet about the whole situation in detail. My career as an Airman of the United States Military was over. They are going to put me out of the service with a dishonorable discharge. There wasn't anything for me to do but ask to see a lawyer. Right when I was going to give up hope the phone rings. It was the investigating detective wanting me to come down to the police station. The commander told me that I had five days before my court martial and he was going to set up an appointment for me the following day to see a lawyer. Then he dismissed me.

I rushed down to the precinct.

"I have good news for you, Roland," the Detective said. "All charges have been dropped. You are free to go."

I was pleased and very shocked. I asked him what had happened. The Detective told me that Janet had a scamming ring full of insurance agents in City-Wide branches all over the state. I had to hand it to her. It was a good scam. She would use a house that one of the agents owned and invite someone over to see all the nice things in there and then she and some of the other agents would rob that house and collect the insurance money. Of course to make it work they would use a military person for the fingerprints so it would be easy to trace and that person would have to deal with the punishment set by the government, which is jail time in Leavenworth. If the robbery didn't stick the adultery would. Either charge meant jail time. After he told me that, I asked him how she got caught? The detective told me that the reason she got caught was because a guy who she pulled that scam on got out of prison not too long ago and decided to come back to visit her. When he heard that she was being investigated for the same thing he was convicted five years ago for, he knew he had been scammed. That's when he turned her in. We are still trying to get the rest of the agents involved in this ring, but rest assured we will get them. After thanking the detective I had to go and try to regain my life—if it wasn't too late.

I drove right back to work to tell my supervisor and commander the news hoping that would set everything straight. But I was wrong. I tried calling my wife to tell her the news, but she still needed her time away from me to think about what happened. Even though some of my friends also had girlfriends on the side, and had so for years, I was the only one who ever got caught. Their wives wouldn't let them be around me anymore. I couldn't even call their houses. My only hope was that I would still have my military career so I can always start anew. That too was wishful thinking. In the military's eyes, the adultery had to be dealt with, and it was dealt with very quickly. The military made an example out of me. In two weeks time I was in Leavenworth serving two years for adultery. I was thinking at the very least I would be dishonorably discharged, but I was wrong. They put my uniforms, as well as my civilian clothes, in storage. Now I wear a uniform with orange stripes down both sides of it. The good thing about all of this is that when my time is done here I will get my old job back, but minus 1 stripe. I was young so it didn't really matter to me.

CHAPTER 5

I wrote my wife every week and in return she sent me pictures of our son once a month. She never wrote me any letters just pictures.

One day the women chow hall on their wing of the prison caught fire. No one was hurt, but now we had to share our chow hall. This was a blessing in disguise. I haven't seen a female in a little over a year. My cellmate, whose name I won't mention, loved telling me stories. I don't know if they were true, but they were entertaining. It took them a month to repair the damage done to their chow hall, and I enjoyed every meal. There was this one girl I couldn't keep my eyes off of and my cellmate knew this. On the night before the women chow hall was to reopen the old man who was my cellmate asked me if I wanted to hear a story about her.

"Of course I do. What do you got for me? Because if I can't get my wife back I'm going to try to make some moves on her when we get out," I said.

"She's in for the long haul just like me," he said laughing.

What a disappointment. I flopped on my bed and stared at the ceiling while he began to tell me the story he titled "Tech School Blues" The Military Life Of Tina Wallace.

This story starts off on a military installation in northern California. Life as a new GI of the United States military can be pretty hard if you are not use to adapting to your surroundings. It isn't for everybody as I am about to tell you. This is a fraction of the life of Tina Wallace.

The door opens to the dorm room as Tina walks in. As soon as the door shuts, a voice comes from the back of the room.

"Hello, my name is Karen. Karen Wheeler, your roommate for the next couple of months. What's you name?" she said.

"I'm Tina Wallace, but just call me Tina," she responds. Karen nods as she helps Tina bring her luggage in the room.

"I'm kind of hungry," Karen says. "When you get situated do you want to go to Burger King with me?"

"Sure. I'll be done in a minute," Tina replies. Shortly after that they decide to walk instead of riding the shuttle to Burger King. This would give them time to get to know each other.

As they walk, they begin to talk about their lives.

"I'll go first," Karen said. "As you can see I am Caucasian. You already know my name. I'm 19 years old. I'm what they call a military brat. This is the only life I know. I'm the first female in my family to join the military. I don't know anything about the streets. That's because I've spent my life on military installations. I'm studying to be a psychiatrist. I like to help solve people's problems. So if you ever need a solution I'm the person to talk to."

"By the way you're dressed and carrying yourself, it seems like your family did pretty good in the military," Tina says. "Why didn't you just go to school and get your degree instead of joining up?"

Karen stopped walking and looked at Tina.

"You think I joined because I wanted to? This was my duty for the family. At least in four years I'll get my degree and would have served my country at the same time. That will be it for me. If I need more schooling by then, I won't have far to go. So what's your story Tina?" she asked.

They begin to walk again. Tina begins to tell her story.

"My life isn't half as pretty as yours, Karen. To start with, my mother ran out on my father and me. I've been living with him up until he died of cancer four months ago," she said.

"I'm sorry," Karen replied as she pats Tina on the back.

"Thanks, but he did his best to raise me as a respectful, God fearing female. I'm proud of him for that. Now even though he is gone, I have to make his spirit proud. I told him that I would be known someday. Being broke with no place to go, I saw a recruitment sign and said, what do I have to lose? I didn't know I had to take a test before I could join. You know that ASVAB test? My scores were so high that they told me that I could pick basically any job in the service. They also said I would have a better chance at being what I want to be, and that is an Oncologist, you know a cancer doctor. To accomplish that feat would make my father proud," Tina said.

As she finished up her story, they were walking into Burger King and it was time for them to order.

They placed their order and get their food, then they looked for a table to sit down. There's a girl sweeping the floor. Karen tries to walk around her, but the girl sweeping the floor turns around too fast and knocks Karen's tray of food on the floor.

"Oh, I'm sorry," the sweeper says.

"I'm sorry? You need to go and get her some more food," Tina said.

"That's ok, I'll just go and buy some more food," Karen says.

"No! I won't let you do that. She should buy you some more food," Tina yells.

There was a moment of silence. Then Tina goes up to the counter, but not before telling Karen to sit and watch her food. Three minutes pass by and then comes Tina with some food for Karen.

"How did you get that?" Karen says surprisingly. "Don't you worry about it my friend. Let's eat. In fact, let's take our food and eat it in the room. Here, you can put your food in this bag," Tina said.

The two girls decide to take the shuttle back to the dorm. The manager of Burger King comes running out looking for Tina and Karen, but he didn't see them.

Meanwhile 1,742 miles away, somewhere in Texas, there is a young man with two weeks left before he graduates from basic training. This is the first step of many before embarking into a career as a service man. From out of an office comes the order, "Airman Casey front and center!"

"Man, what now?" Joe whispers to himself.

Joe goes to the office from where the order came from. It's his drill sergeant. Joe stands at attention, and tells his drill sergeant he is reporting as ordered. The drill sergeant looks him over.

"Joe, I have a new job for you. You are now my dorm chief. If this flight of Airmen graduates together, it will be because you made it happen," says the drill sergeant. "You are they liaison. Any question they might have will go through you first before coming to me. Do you understand me, Airman Casey?"

Joe snaps to attention again and replies, "sir, yes sir!" The drill sergeant instructs Joe to get the flight ready for their wall locker inspection.

1,742 miles north from here is a new day in the military for an Airman named Tina Wallace. Today is the first day of Tech school. The classroom is full. Tina is surprised, so she stands in the corner.

"Excuse me, young Airman, why are you still standing?" the teacher of the class asks.

Tina looked up into the teacher's eyes and she just felt like melting. He is so fine, Tina thinks to herself. With a big smile she tells the teacher that she didn't have a seat. The teacher, who goes by the name of Major Johnson, saw how nervous Tina was with being in his class, so he made arrangements, though it was hard to add another desk to his already full classroom. All through class all Tina could think about was how the Major made room for her to stay in his class.

When class was over she stayed back to thank him.

"Major Johnson, I would like to say thank you for keeping me in your class," Tina says.

Then out of nowhere she gives him a hug. He is shocked, but he didn't seem to mind it at the time.

"Bye, Major Johnson. See you tomorrow," said Tina as she ran out of the room glowing.

Shortly after Tina left, the teacher from across the hall came in Major Johnson's room and told him that he better watch himself. Your troop has a crush on you and that isn't good, she tells him. The Major chuckled and said that she was just happy to be in the military.

Meanwhile, back in the dorm, Karen comes in the room after dinner and tells Tina that people were talking about a boy being overheard on the phone. He was telling who ever he was talking to that he was gay, and joining the military was the only way to fool his father.

"I can't believe anybody would be that stupid to say stuff like that on the phone," Tina said.

"I know, and his stupidity has earned him a one-way ticket back home," Karen replied. "What was that they tell us when we joined? Oh yeah, don't ask don't tell," she said, laughing out loud.

One week has gone by and Tina has told Karen that she likes the Major. Then she told her that today she would ask him to tutor her so she could spend more time with him. She warned her to be careful, because if she got caught fraternizing she could get kicked out of the military.

CHAPTER 6

Back in San Antonio, Texas, the trumpets sound. It's graduation and Joe leads his troops to the ceremony. This is just another typical military ceremony with different faces. Now the new graduates pack their clothes and get ready to go to their highly respected Technical school. There are some troops who cry and some that are scared of what is to come in their immediate future. Joe is just happy that boot camp was finally over.

A few days go by and the tutoring sessions are going the way Tina had planned. One day after the tutoring session, Tina leans over and gives the Major a good-bye kiss on the cheek. The Major looks surprised but not alarmed.

Later on that night she comes in her room singing a love song.

"What are you so happy about?" Karen asks.

"Guess who I just kissed?" Tina says as she smiles.

"I know you did not kiss Major Johnson. Please say it isn't so," Karen says jumping up out of her chair.

"Yes ma'am I did, and he didn't even pull away," she replies.

Karen told Tina that she had better slow down because she can get into real big trouble. Tina still didn't listen to Karen's advice. Instead she started singing again and got into the shower.

Back at Major Johnson's apartment, a phone call is being made. The Major decides to call one of his buddies.

"Hello! Yeah this is J.J.," he says.

"What's up man?" the voice on the other side says. "How is the military treating you?"

"I can't complain," the Major says. "Listen Carl, I got this female student who has a crush on me. I don't know exactly what I should do. She kissed me good-bye today. No one saw, but if I get caught with this delicate situation I will go from Major Johnson to convict Johnson. Help me out man."

Carl clears his throat and tells the Major to be careful and think about his future not hers. The Major agrees with his long time friend and they continue to talk about everything else that is going on in their lives.

Back in the dorm room of Tina and Karen, the shower is running. Tina is still in the shower and Karen makes a call home. You can guess that the topic of conversation was about Tina, and you will be right. Karen's mother told her to turn her in. That way nothing can be blamed on her.

"Honey, I know that is your friend, but you don't want her actions to bring you down, do you?" Karen's mother said.

"No mom, but being her friend I feel that I should help her," Karen replies.

Karen's mother insists that she turn her in. Karen hears Tina getting out of the shower so she tells her mother she needs to go. She tells her mother she will keep her posted on the situation. They say their good-byes and Karen hangs up and gets in the bed.

Outside of the dorm, Joe finally arrives at Technical school, and all the students pile off the bus. Everybody checks in with the dorm monitor to get his or her rooms. Joe gets his key and settles in his room. He has a room all to himself because earlier the other guy occupying the room graduated on to his permanent duty base. A couple of minutes later he hears a girl singing a song that he just happens to like. Joe wonders where the singing is coming from. Then he walks over to the window. It's coming from right below him. Joe moves his bed over to the window so he could hear the singing better. After a while he drifts off to sleep to the singing of the girl from downstairs.

The next morning Joe was eating breakfast in the chow hall when from around the corner he hears the voice that had put him to sleep the night before. It was Tina and Karen coming into the chow hall to eat breakfast. Joe could hardly contain himself. He waits until they get their food and sits down. He has his eye on Tina, but he doesn't know if it was her or Karen singing. Joe makes his move.

"Hello, my name is Joe," he says. The girls both introduce themselves. Joe gazes at Tina and asks them who was singing last night. He tells them that it was one of his favorite songs and that he is staying in the room right above them.

Karen smiles and then she points at Tina. Joe is impressed that a female can sing so well and have such beauty. They all chat with one another until the girls finished their breakfast. After breakfast everyone in the chow hall lines up in their respected classes and march to school. While getting in formation Karen told Tina that she thinks that Joe likes her.

"Oh girl, you know that it's the Major and me," Tina says. "You can have Joe. I don't have time for him. I'll see you after school."

Days go bye and everything is going as planned as far as Tina is concerned. Every day Joe eats breakfast, lunch, and dinner with Tina whether Karen is there or not. Every day Tina tells Joe that she is interested in someone else.

"For the last two weeks I've tried to get with you and you tell me that you are interested in someone else," Joe says. "If you are so interested in this person why haven't I seen you with anybody other than Karen or me?"

Tina pushes her tray back and before she leaves the chow hall she turns around and tells Joe to mind his own business.

One day, five minutes before class was over for Tina, some flowers were delivered and everyone in the class made kissing sounds. Tina was smiling until the flower man said the flowers were for Major Johnson. Tina stayed after class to find out who sent these flowers to him. The Major told her that they were from his fiancée. Tina blew up.

"How could you do this to me?" she yells. "All this time we spent together. I kissed you. None of that means anything to you does it?"

The Major puts his flowers down and tells Tina that they are teacher and student—no more, no less.

"You should have not kissed me," the Major says. "We are both adults here and we are both in the military. You have to learn how to keep your military bearing, airman. I'm sorry if you have mistaking our tutoring sessions for something else, but I'm an Officer and you are an enlisted Airman. What you want can't happen anyway. That would be fraternization."

The Major tells Tina that she is attractive but young and need to find an enlisted Airman to spend her time with. Then he proceeds to tell her that he thinks it would be better if he transferred her to another class. Tina apologized and pleaded to stay in his class. She agreed to no more tutoring sessions and no flirting with him. Major Johnson thought for a second and agreed.

"Go back to your dorm, Tina, and all this will be forgotten," the Major said.

Tina went back to the dorm crying. She tried to eat but she just cried all over her food. Joe came in the chow hall and saw her crying. He sits down next to her.

"What's the matter, my friend?" asks Joe.

"I don't feel like talking right now, Joe," she replied.

"O.k.," Joe says. "Here is my number. If you need to talk to somebody, it doesn't matter what time it is, you give me a call."

Tina puts the number in her pocket. Joe pats her on the back and tells her that everything is going to be all right. Then he smiles and begins to sing the song he had heard the first night he got there. It was the song from the girl downstairs, which just happened to be Tina. She looks up at him with tears in her eyes and smiles back at him as he walked out of the chow hall.

After Tina nibbles a little more on her food she goes to her room where she finds Karen ironing her uniform.

"What's wrong, roomie?" Karen says as she looks up from her ironing.

Tina flops down on her bed and tells Karen what had happen with the Major. Karen was relieved that it was over, but she acted like she felt sorry for her. Then she told Karen that she was going to get with Joe to make the Major jealous. She says she is going to call Joe before she goes to sleep.

Joe is studying when his phone rings. He is surprised that it was Tina. They chat on the phone until Joe notices Tina dosing off. He thanks her for calling and tells her she needs to get some rest. In the morning, they eat together and laugh all through breakfast. After school Tina waits for Joe to get out of class. When Joe comes out he is shocked to see her there. She sees Major Johnson standing at the door, so she runs up to Joe and gives him a big kiss. She thought that the Major would be jealous but when she looked back at the door he was gone. It didn't work. Joe is really thinking that Tina likes him now so he starts to buy her things. She just loves it. She never spoke to the Major out side of school, but she kept on trying to make him jealous with Joe. Poor Joe, he was in the middle of this silly game that Tina is playing and doesn't even know it. Every other day the Major got a call from his fiancée. Tina tried not to get upset, but her jealously stuck out like a sore thumb.

One day she thought to herself that enough is enough. During class she asked to be excused to go to the bathroom, but instead she went outside to the parking lot where the Major parks his car. When she got there she looked around to see if anybody was out there. She was alone. She took out a knife and slashed all the tires on his car and went back to class thinking she taught him a great lesson not to mess with her.

Later that day her and Joe walked to the BX, a military shopping center, when they heard a horn honk. When they turned around it was the Major in his car—with new tires—saying hello to them. The Major was happy that she had found somebody else. He smiled at Tina and she gave a not so convincing smile back. She couldn't believe that he got the car fixed that quickly. She thought to herself, maybe cutting his tires wasn't enough. Tomorrow she is going to put sugar in his tank.

"Are you all right Tina?" Joe says. "You looked as if you were somewhere else."

"Yes, sweetie, I'm just fine," she says.

The next day Tina asked to be excused again. This time she put sugar in his tank. This will fix him and get him mad for sure, she thought. She skipped back to class and was cheerful the whole daylong. The Major asked her why she was so happy today. She said that she was just in a sweet mood.

Class was over now and Joe came to get her. They walked back to the dorm. Joe wanted to know what time did she want to eat, and she told him to eat without her tonight.

"I'm not eating tonight. I'll call you after I study for my final exam," she says and waits until Joe goes upstairs to his room then makes a mad dash back to the school building. When she gets there she is out of breath and the Major car is gone. She is shocked that he is gone. He should be out here trying to start his car. Now she is starting to despise him, and to make it worse, the Major—the very next day—offered her and Joe a ride back to the dorm after school. Him acting as if nothing has been happening to his car was driving Tina over the wall.

Well time has gone by as it always does. Karen and Tina have graduated. Karen tells Tina that she didn't think that she was going to make it because of her obsession with the Major. Tina smiles at her and thanks her for being her friend through that whole ordeal. They give each other a hug and say their last good-byes. Then they go their separate ways. They will have new adventures and new friends on their first permanent duty station.

CHAPTER 7

Now that Tina is at her new base, she can hopefully put the past behind her and move on. That's not likely though. Instead she can't get the Major out of her head. She has no problem with Joe. She cut it off with him right after she graduated. They are still friends. Tina is trying to think of a way to see the Major one more time. Then she decides to give him a call. Her timing was perfect. When he got the word during class that he had a call he knew it was his fiancée.

"Hello sweetie! I miss you so much," he said.

"I miss you also, but too bad it had to take me leaving for you to realize that," Tina says with a chuckle.

"Who is this?" he says puzzled.

Click. Tina hangs up the phone. She is very mad now because she realized that he thought that she was his fiancée.

Joe is sitting in his room thinking about Tina. Then he goes downstairs to sit in the lobby. Shortly after, a guy comes in the dorm and he is passing out flyers. He gives one to Joe and then he leaves. Joe reads the flyer and the flyer reads "Big Bash for Major Johnson." After reading this all he can think about is trying to get Tina to come back to go with him to the bash. So Joe runs to his room to call her. He gives her a call, and when she answers and hears that it is Joe, she acts as if she is so surprised to hear From Joe. She was hoping that it was Major Johnson calling her back, but it wasn't.

"I hope you're not mad at me for calling, but the base locator patched me through to you," he said.

They chatted for a while. She told him about her job and he told her how she missed her. Joe paused for a response, but all he got was silence. Then he broke the silence by asking Tina to go with him to Major Johnson's Banquet. Tina thought that this is her chance to go back to see the Major one more time.

"Sure, I'll be glad to go. When is it?" she replies. Joe tells her that the bash is Saturday at 8 p.m. They agree to meet at the ballroom on this base at 8:30 p.m.

"I only got five days to find a dress, so I'll talk to you later," she says. That concluded their conversation.

Joe was happy to be seeing Tina again and that is his thought as he drifts off to sleep. Tina was happy also. Not because she was going to see Joe again, but because she was going to try and have one more crack at Major Johnson. Tina takes out a picture of her Technical school class and looks at The Major.

"I vow to you, that if you're not mine on Saturday you will definitely not be hers," she says softly. She gives the picture a kiss and puts it away.

Days go bye and it is now Saturday at 7:15pm. Tina steps off of the plane and is the happiest she's been since she could remember. She walks through the corridor to the taxi stand when she looks down and notices Major Johnson on the cover of the Military Times. The headline reads "The USAF would like to congratulate Major Johnson on being a newlywed." She opens it up and reads on. A wedding reception tonight at 8:00pm, she says to herself. She thought this was just a banquet, not a wedding reception.

Tina turns around and runs to the ticket counter crying. She asks for a ticket for the next plane going back where she just came from. While waiting for her plane a guy approaches her. He appears to be some kind of bum just hanging around. He asks her if she's all right and if he could help her in any way. Tina tells him to get a life, and then spits in his face.

Time goes by and it is now 8:56pm. Joe is getting impatient. He wonders where she is and knows that she didn't take the money he sent her Western Union and spent it on something else. Joe waited and waited, but Tina was a no-show.

The next day, later that evening Joe gets a call. It's Tina telling Joe how sorry she is about last night. She tells him that she had an emergency at the last minute and couldn't call him.

"Are you all right?" Joe asks.

"Yeah, it turned out to be nothing after all, imagine that," Tina says. "So how was it?"

Joe clears his throat. "My cousin was murdered in the parking lot," Joe says. "It appeared that she was mugged. I feel so bad, because it was my fault."

Tina cuts him off and asks Joe how was it his fault. Joe told Tina that his cousin was going to the car to get a gift for him that his mother had told her to give him.

"Instead of enjoying that night I begged her to go get my gift. You know what's funny?" he asked.

Tina says she doesn't believe anything could be funny about that situation. But Joe told her that all this time he didn't know that her old teacher Major Johnson was marrying his cousin. Tina was in shock. She couldn't believe it.

"Joe, I am so sorry that happened," Tina said feeling sorry for him. Joe tells her that the Military gave him two weeks off. Tina has an idea. Tina asks him to come see her. Joe thinks for a second and then he tells her that he will come.

"I got to go Tina. I have to call home and tell my parents that they still don't have any suspects here," he says.

Tina tells him to keep his head up and she can't wait to see him.

Joe calls his mother and tells her the latest about the situation. After he talked to his mother he called up Major Johnson. They talk for a while then they agree to meet tomorrow so they could get to know each other.

The next day they go for a walk through the park. Joe tells the Major that he was family now, so if he needed anything he could count on him. They talk about Joe's cousin for a while, then the conversation turned to Tina.

The Major told Joe that she was a good troop in the beginning, until she found out that he was engaged.

"Man, let me tell you something," Major Johnson says. "If you are still dealing with her be careful for two reasons. For one, after I set her straight about me being engaged and her and I being only teacher and student, she blew up at me. It was as if she was someone else. For two, she is a suspect to your cousin's murder."

Joe is surprised at everything that he is hearing. Joe tells him that he still keeps in touch with her. In fact, she was supposed to go to the reception, but she never showed up, Joe tells the major.

"I'm supposed to go see her for a few days after I make my statement to the investigating detective tomorrow. The Military gave me a couple of weeks off," Joe adds.

As they were walking back to the dorm, the Major told Joe to make sure he tells the investigating detective about Tina when he makes his statement.

"You're not hooked on her, are you?" asked the Major.

"I was a month ago," he responds.

A few days have now passed and Major Johnson gives Joe a ride to the military airport terminal. He tells Joe as he is boarding the plane to be careful and if he needs anything to give him a call.

In a matter of hours Joe is giving Tina a hug. Tina tells him he looks kind of tired. She was going to show him around, but instead she decides to just take him to her home so he can rest. They pull up to her apartment and Joe is curious to how she was able to get an apartment being just an Airman Basic. No sooner than Joe can finish his thought, Tina tells him how. She tells him that she told her First Shirt, the liaison between enlisted personnel and officers, that it was too noisy in the dorm and she couldn't study her Promotion Fitness Examination (PFE) to make rank.

Joe puts his cloths in Tina's room.

"Where is your bathroom?" Joe asked. She shows him where it is and then goes in to the kitchen to get something to drink.

CHAPTER 8

While Joe is in the bathroom he sees a familiar piece of jewelry wrapped around a teddy bear. He picks it up. Just as he thought, it was the bracelet that his mother had sent to him by his cousin.

"What's taking you so long? You all right Joe?" Tina asked.

Joe's heart begins to beat faster.

"Yeah, here I come," Joe replies.

He puts the bracelet in his pocket and comes out of the bathroom in complete shock at his findings. He lies on her bed and tries to piece this thing together, but before he can, in walks Tina.

"You looked like you've just seen a ghost," Tina said. "I'm just tired, that's all," he says. "When are you coming to bed?"

"I have to wash these dishes right quick," she replied.

Joe is laying on the bed plotting up a plan. After Tina finishes the dishes she comes in, kisses Joe, and gets in the bed. As Tina settles in the bed, Joe asks her where she got the bracelet on the teddy bear in the bathroom. She chuckles and tells him that she had it so long that she doesn't remember. Tina soon after that drifts off to sleep. Joe acted as if he was a sleep, but he had other plans. He sneaks out of bed and calls the Major. As soon as the Major picked up the phone, Joe started telling him everything that happened and where she stayed. The Major told Joe to get out of there and wait for the authorities, but Joe told him that she was a sleep and doesn't know that he knows anything.

They get off the phone and Joe sneaks back in bed. He thought that Tina was a sleep, but she was not.

The next morning Joe wakes up to see Tina standing over him. Joe is startled.

"Did I scare you?" she asked. "I was just wondering what you did with my bracelet."

Joe is lying on his back. Then he tells her to cut the crap.

"You know what, Tina? I thought you were something special until I found my bracelet that I never got from my cousin in your bathroom," Joe says. "I know you killed my cousin and you are going to pay for it."

Tina smiles.

"How am I going to pay for it when you are going to be the only one that will ever know?" she says.

With that, Tina pulls out a butcher knife that she had hidden in one of her hands behind her back. Before Joe can move she drives the knife deep in his upper right chest.

Joe falls on the floor and she takes off running for the front door. When she opens the door she sees a couple of guns pointed at her.

"Freeze! Don't move. You are under arrest," an officer said. She drops the butcher knife on the floor and surrenders. The police rush in to find Joe bleeding very badly on the floor. They call the paramedics for him. Shortly after the call they arrive and take Joe to the hospital on base. The police turn Tina over to the military authorities.

They held Tina for a month in confinement. That is how long it took for them to get a court-martial date. The day of the court-martial has come and Tina is constantly saying that they have nothing on her. When asked what she had to say about the stabbing, she told them that Joe was trying to rape her. Then they called in a MACC terminal security guard, whose job it is to be undercover and keep an eye out for any suspicious people or packages. Tina is feeling confident about her case until she looks up and sees who she thought was a bum at the MACC terminal, the one she spit on. He gets on the stand with all the evidence at hand, and tells the people what and how it happened on that evening.

"On the night in question, Tina flew into town. She rented a car and went to the crime scene. On arrival, she sees the bride going to her car. That's when the altercation took place where the bride ended up murdered. The only thing that was missing was the bracelet that Joe Casey found a month ago in the bathroom of the accused. There were words on the back that read, "We are proud of you Airman Casey, Love Mom and Dad". The bride that died that night was the cousin of Joe Casey. She was going to the car to get him the gift that his mother had sent to him by his cousin. He never got it, because the accused took it from the murder scene. I believe that she didn't mean to kill her, but when she realized she did she panicked and tried to make it look like a mugging. Then she returned back at the MACC terminal after changing her bloodied cloths and took the next hop back from which she had came. I have here the bloody dress she threw away in the Dumpster in the back of the terminal," he said.

Next it was the Major's turn. He told them everything from the tutoring sessions to the things that happened to his car. Then finally it was Joe's turn. By the time he finished she was in tears.

After all the testimonies were heard by the members of the court-martial, the judge asked Tina to stand up. Once she was standing he asked her, "How do you plead"? There was a pause.

"Guilty, your honor, guilty of it all," Tina said. The judge told her she will have her sentencing one-week from today, and drops the gavel.

"Take her away," he says as she is crying out loud. As the officers took her out of the courtroom she fell to her knees, looked up and said "sorry to disappoint you father."

"Now that girl was crazy. Do you think that you still want to hook up with her?" the old man said.

"I think I'll concentrate on getting back with my wife," I said.

And that was exactly what I did. I told the old man that the cruelest thing I ever did to a female was right before I joined up. I had her and her family believing that we were getting married when I got out of basic training, but I used them to store my car and clothing. My wife to be didn't have anywhere to keep my stuff. When I came back I got my stuff from the girl's family and told them that I was taking them all out for dinner where I was going to propose to their daughter. I told them I had to drop my stuff off at the port and would be back at 6pm. That was the last time I saw or spoke to them. I know they would kill me if they ever saw me again, but they won't see me again. They were good church folk, but very gullible.

I heard that they had told the members of the church and told the minister to get ready for a ceremony. I wonder what they told them when I didn't show?

"Females are the death of men. Be careful, young man. You do know the saying about a woman scorned don't you?" the old man asked.

"Yeah, but I can't dwell on the past. I have to concentrate on getting my wife back," I responded.

After sending countless letters to my wife I received a letter back stating that she was coming to see me and if I could convince her, she would not file for divorce. I had two weeks until she arrived. I called every family member on both sides to seek help in saving my marriage. I even called the preacher of our church who married us. He had a good idea. His idea was to come to the prison the same day that my wife was to show up and give us both some counseling. I knew that this would work. I made sure I looked my best and had my words in order.

The day had come and the three of us were sitting in the visitor lounge. We talked for an hour. That may not seem like a long time to you, but to me it felt like we were talking for days. I begged for my wife to take me back, saying all the things I knew she wanted to hear. The guard had come to escort them out, but the preacher told the guard that he had to say a prayer for us first. I can't remember what the preacher said in his prayer, but when he was finished I remember the tears flowing down both me and my wife's face. That was the new start I had prayed for ever since that dreadful day at my court martial hearing. My wife had always had dreams of being a nurse. I promised her that I would make sure that she got her schooling when I get out. The difference between military prison and prison on the out side, is that the military will wash your slate clean after you do your time in certain circumstances. In my case I lost my ranking, family and two years out of my life, but I'm not complaining because I'm getting my wife back and in time I'll get my rank back.

CHAPTER 9

When I got out of Leavenworth, I had to make good on my promises to my wife. One thing was to help her get back into college. The military was good at getting you an education, and my wife took advantage of the help she received. She was a straight "A" student while studying in the nursing career field. Once the Military get wind of that news they offered all kind of grants, loans, and even an offer to help her get through school without paying. Their offer was simple. All she had to do was sign up for five years as a head nurse in one of the Military hospitals once she graduated and they would pay for the rest of her schooling plus give her a $5,000 bonus. Of course she jumped on it, but the bad thing is that I introduced her to the military and now she was going to out rank me.

She is the smartest female you could imagine as long as she was in those schoolbooks, but once she stepped out in the streets there were no smarts at all. She had next to no common sense. Our house was always a mess. To let her tell the story, we ate out most of the time because of her studying, not being able to cook that well or just not feeling like cooking. I did all the cleaning in the house and even cleaned after her. I have to hand it to her, she was so scared of getting kicked out of base housing that she did the cutting of the grass. I'm glad that my mother was taking care of our child until we got back on our feet, but even still enough is enough. Now she is doing this Military medical plan thing. After 3 years of her laziness and dirtiness I had enough. I was feeling that she was acting this way because of the trouble

I was in, you know like being in prison and all. Her excuse was that her schooling was taking a lot out of her and that she was over what had happen in the pass. That was a relief. In fact she didn't even want me to bring up the fact that I spent two years in prison for adultery. She said that it only made her mad.

I was putting in fourteen hour-six days a week at work, and I still had time for her as well as keep up the cleanliness of the house. That was it, if I was going to keep my sanity I had to pick up a hobby that I will tell you about a little later.

Whenever Paula came home I would wait a half hour or so and then I would go and tend to my new hobby. Whenever I was finished I would come home and the fighting would commence. I know she thought I was having another affair, but it wasn't like that. This hobby of mine kept me feeling good about being in the military, and I knew she wouldn't believe that. Anyway, somewhere around 2 months time I went out to dabble with my hobby and felt as if I was being watched, and I was. One night I came home to find my wife sitting on the couch with her arms folded. I asked her what was the matter. She told me that she knew what I've been up to. Paula knew everything. Apparently she had borrowed someone's car to follow me. I had no choice but to tell her. Since she knows I might as well tell you what I do on my spare time. It would seem that my time in prison should have kept me on the straight and narrow, but it didn't. I was able to suppress my appetite for women for now, so my hobby had nothing to do with females. I'm a big fan of electronics, but to keep up with the rapid growth of electronics you need money and that I did not have. I was spending countless hours trying to figure out how I could get some money to buy the latest gadgets, and then it hit me. I can pawn things around the house that we weren't using anymore. That helped for a while until I ran out of things to pawn. Where we live on base there are a lot of people who work at the same job at the same time. You can walk down any given street in the residential part of the base and it would be a ghost town.

That gave me an idea that took me back to my college days. When I was in college my cousin and I had this scheme we used to do. I would bring girls home and they thought I lived alone. Meanwhile my cousin is hiding in one of the closets. I would get the girl to get comfortable on the living room couch. Once she put her purse down I would invite her into the bedroom. Two thing would either happen: my cousin would sneak out of the closet, take what ever money she had in her purse and then leave without her even knowing; or, if she spent the night he would take her keys to her place and rob her blind. We never got caught doing that. It was perfect. These unsuspected females would never know what happened and they would never find out. That's when I said if it worked back then it would definitely work now, especially when military people feel so protected on base. They leave their doors unlocked, keys in the car, and sometimes they go on vacation with their home unsecured. Imagine this, we as military personnel travel all over the world so you can imagine all the neat stuff that is in these types of houses. So this is what I started doing. I would wait for a function to take place. See, in the military they like to think that everyone is family. They always try to get you to spend time together with your co-workers outside of work. This is the perfect opportunity to go to work, if you know what I mean. To go to work the way I mean is to play cat burglar. I cased a lot of people's homes and waited for them to go to a squadron function, out to dinner and a movie, or even on a vacation. I know how long they're going to be gone so I just take my time and steal every thing I want. If you case the right people you can really get some good stuff. I have this friend that owns a pawnshop. I can't put his business out in the streets, but let's just say he owes me big, and for that, everything I stole I would sell to him and he would fence it for me. We had a system that worked and it was good.

After telling my wife that, she was shocked and confused. She said she didn't think I could be that diabolical. That's when I told her that no man tells all he knows. I think hearing all of this made her really horny because that night we had the best sex we've ever had. I asked her if she wanted to feel the rush of being a cat burglar, to help me get more stuff? She was kind of weary at first, but when she felt the rush of instant gratification I couldn't control her. She was better at casing people than I was. She had this idea of having a study group and while they studied I would be robbing the person of the week. Each person would host a study group at their respected homes all the while my wife is checking out the place and getting the layout. It was going great, and so was our relationship. Who cared about the messy house? We had so much extra money coming in that we hired a maid service to come in twice a week to clean. In some strange way this hobby was bringing us close again like we were in the beginning.

Then came some of the close calls. For example, this one family went to the park, but left one of their daughters behind. Locks were never a problem for me seeing that I'm a locksmith in the Military. That's what I do. I work on security locks. So I guess I can thank the military for my skills. Seeing that the close calls kept coming more and more frequent, we decided to take a break. We only knew so many people and we had to spread it out so no one would suspect anything. I started showing my face at these squadron functions and my wife took over making the runs. She would even make the drops at the pawnshop.

Let me tell you a little about Hector who ran the pawnshop. Hector is from Mexico and he dreamed of living in America.

His father left Hector when he was 10 years old to make a way for the family to come over. The only thing was that his father never came back for them. When his father died he left Hector the Pawn Shop. Hector was 18 when he came to America to take over the shop. When I first got out of prison I use to buy used music CD's from him. Then one day he asked me if I could get him some old Military gear to send back to his people in Mexico. Apparently they pay top dollar for military surplus. From there he told me that in return if I ever come across anything that I wanted to sell, he'd sell it for me for a small price. I never gave it much thought until now.

After a good six months of robbing and stealing I felt that it was time to let it go. We had taken as much stuff for us not to be rich, but for us to be comfortable. My wife got mad at me, because she was hooked. She didn't want to stop. I told her that I would go with her one last time and then we would have to cut all ties with Hector.

It's always the last time that gets you. We planned our last night of stealing to take place in two weeks. I felt like a professional football player when they know that their career is coming to an end. Then the time had come. We prepared ourselves as we always have before. I was a little nervous. Taking that time off made me realize that I was a lucky man. Our hobby paid off our $55,000 debt. I thought to myself that this was going to be our last job of this kind; my wife was going to be graduating soon, and then we could concentrate on having another baby. Thinking of these things put my mind at ease. My wife had cased the perfect place. The family was on a vacation and so we had all night to pick what we wanted. The father of this home was a local doctor and the wife, of course, worked in the hospital. They have two teenage boys who have a lot of electronic gadgets. That stuff always brings in good cash. Everything went as planned.

My wife got bold with it. As soon as we walked into the house from the back she jumped on my back and started undressing me. She seduced me on those people's dining room table. After our sex romp in someone else's house we began what would be our last caper. After taking as much as we could possibly take, we headed to Hector's one last time.

I called him as we were pulling up to his place. He greeted us as he looked over our stuff. I told him that this was the last time that he would see us. It didn't seem to faze him much.

"You know the drill, Roland. Put the goods in the back of the shop," Hector said. "I'll go get your money".

As I loaded the goods in the back of the pawnshop, Paula went inside to go to the bathroom, so I told her to get the money from Hector and meet me across the street at the Seven Eleven. I finished putting the goods in the back of the pawnshop and went across the street to get a frosty. I waited for Paula over there for a good long time. It felt like forever, which it always does when you're doing wrong, but actually it was about 20 minutes. I wondered what is taking Paula so long. I'm getting impatient waiting at the truck, so I go to see what's the hold up. As I walk into the pawnshop, I hear Hector's office door close. I just happen to look through the slits of his blinds to see my wife kissing him, the pawnshop broker. I was so stunned that I dropped my now empty cup on the floor. Before I could pick it up, here they come out of the office.

"Let's go honey I have the money," she said to me.

I couldn't even look at her. I just got up and started walking back to the truck. I know I did her wrong and I even went to prison over it, but why would she take me back just to cheat on me? On the way I'm thinking to myself whether she knows that I saw her? Hector has the nerve to say to me "thanks for everything, Roland. We have got to do more business together sometime." That guy had a lot of nerve, but I can't blame him for Paula's actions.

It was a long, quiet ride home. Then Paula asks me if anything is wrong? Of course I told her no, because I'm in scheming mode now. She tried to get me to do more jobs, but I now know that I need to stop the madness. I'm in the military, for crying out loud. It took days upon days to figure out what I was going to do to them, but I think I have it. I'll set them up. I don't know how long they've been fooling around, but it doesn't matter to me. I caught them and now they will pay, and they would pay dearly.

I still can't believe what has happened. I just knew that my marriage was going to be great with the bills taken care of and all, but I was wrong. What ever is done in the dark will come to the light and I believe that in my heart. This is a major crossroad in my life and I don't know what to do. I now know that I should have walked away from this the moment I found out. Even though I may have stepped out on her once, it doesn't compare to the hurt she caused by stepping out on me after she said she forgave me for cheating on her. Well, now my male ego is hurt and I need some pampering. It took a couple of weeks, but the plan was sweet. I talked to my wife and she still wanted to rob people's homes. So I asked her if she thought she could make a run by herself. I knew she would jump at that opportunity to see Hector again. For all I know, she probably kept seeing him after that night.

CHAPTER 10

Paula was in a house that had a payphone right across the street from it, and I cased it especially for her. I called the officer who lived there from that payphone, and told him what was going to happen to his things after they were to be stolen from his house. Then I went home before he came. Paula didn't even see me. It was hard, but I felt that it had to be done. Three hours later I received a phone call from my wife. She was behind bars and she was using her one phone call to call me. I acted as if I was shocked and told her that I'd be there as quick as I could. I was thinking to myself that now she knows how it felt to be locked up. Later, after I took a shower and grabbed a bite to eat, I showed up at the precinct. I spoke to the clerk and he took me to see my wife. As I walked into the visitor's area I could see the look Paula had on her face. It was of a person who was frightened. My heart dropped into my boots. How could I do this to my wife? This is supposed to be the women that I love, but my ego is still tripping. I got into character and walked up to her. She starts to cry as we embrace.

"Honey, get me out of her," she says to me.

"I'll get you out, but what's going on?" I replied.

She told me that she didn't know. Apparently the police followed her to the pawnshop and when Hector came out to the truck they took both of them in. I told Paula not to say anything until I get a lawyer for her, and for goodness sake, don't say anything about me. If the military thought I had anything to do with this I would be locked up again for good this time around.

I gave her a kiss and on the way out the door I looked back and said to her, "This is what happens when you bite the hand that feeds you." Then I turned my back on her and walked out.

Outside I see Hector leaning against a street light smoking a cigarette. I was surprised that they let him get out so quickly. My wife's life is over and she hasn't even started it yet, I told him. I hope she was worth it. With that I laughed, snatched his cigarette, took a puff and flicked it at him. I turned around and began to walk away. Hector put his hand on my shoulder.

"No man tells all he knows, for one day he may need that extra information to get over." Then Hector started laughing while he put out the cigarette with his foot and went back into the police station. I thought he was a fool for saying what he said. I didn't give him any thought until that night as a lay alone in the bed. Now I'm kind of scared. I'm thinking of ways to make sure my name is clear. This can't get back to the military.

That very next morning I'm at work and then I get called into my commander's office. I don't think or hesitate to go in. In fact I've been doing good at work and I'm thinking that I'm going to get promoted. The reason why I felt that way was because in the office I see my supervisor, his supervisor, and the commander. They had their back towards me. So to get their attention I say proudly, "Sergeant Booker reports as ordered." As they all turn toward me I see what they were doing. They were looking at me on videotape at Hector's place. The tape was of our first meeting where I told Hector what I was into. 45 minutes of incriminating footage. I started backing up slowly until I couldn't go any further, and that was because I backed right into the military police that began reading me my rights. My knees got week and I passed out, but when I came to, I was facing 10 years of hard labor in Fort Leavenworth, Kansas.

It's been three years and all I do is sit in my cell and stay out of trouble. The warden noticed my isolation and moved me to the other side of the prison two cells away from where I use to stay some years back. As I walk around to see the changes to the prison I run into my old cellmate.

"I didn't want to believe it, but here you are in the flesh," he said. "I was wondering why you never wrote me, but now I know why. If you had told me you were coming back I would have saved the bunk in my cell for you. I have a new cellmate now. They call him Sunflower."

By looking at his face I knew he had another story to tell me. I briefly gave him an update of my situation and asked him about his new cellmate. He said he would tell me later. He was late for an appointment.

"Before I go," he continued. "What happened to your wife after getting caught with the pawnbroker?"

"Well, my wife got four years probation for turning states evidence and was stripped of every thing the Military had promised. She also had to pay back all the tuition monies they put toward her schooling. I don't think it mattered much to her. She was going to be graduating in a few weeks with a B.A. in Nursing. I wish her well. As for Hector the pawnbroker, his business license was stripped from him, and seeing that this was his second offence he was deported back to Mexico to keep him from getting his third strike. I felt good about that until I get news that my wife divorced me to married him," I said.

I tell him the worst part of this whole story is that when they tore down Hector's shop that has been in his family for years, they found ancient artifacts. Now he is rich and back in America. I'm glad the warden moved me, because I hated looking out my old cell window just to see the Electronic Expo my ex-wife and Hector built right across the road from the prison.

This was their way of rubbing it in my face, but the joke's on them because it ain't like they're ever going to see my face anyway. I've done three of the ten years and because of my good behavior they put me on a work detail outside the prison walls. I start tomorrow. The warden tells me that if I get a good report after a month I could get paroled by the end of the year.

I told the old man I would catch up with him later. As the old man walked off I turned around and began to wonder about my detail in the morning. That was all I could think about until the next morning when I found myself picking up trash across the street at the Electronics Expo. You should see Hector and Paula's face, because now they get to see mine. I can't stand my life. I've spent just about the same amount of time in military prison as I have in the military. Was it all worth it? I think not. I should have finished college. I joined to get my education and all I got was a prison sentence.

One day after the morning detail I had lunch with my old cellmate and Sunflower. Sunflower was mean looking and talked as if I had something to do with him being locked up. I thought he wanted to fight me. He kept asking me to spar with him. Of course I said no. Then he said if you change your mind I'll be in the gym. He then slid his tray over to me, called me a punk, and told me to dump his tray.

"Do you like sharing a cell with him," I asked the old man.

"He's ok. His mind is on what he is going to do if he ever gets out of here," the old man says. I did some research on him and he has a good story. Let's go watch him work out and on the way over I'll tell you his story, the media called Fixation.

I just loved the way he told stories, this old man. He made you feel as if you was watching it on TV. The old man begins to speak. This is Bob Weathers at a press conference called by the undisputed heavy weight kick boxer of the world, Mr. J. T. Lewis.

"Mr. Lewis, the world awaits your big announcement. This isn't a schedule press conference and I, well we all, would like to know why you have called us here today?"

J. T. clears his throat.

"Well Bob, I called you all here to say that the world has seen my last fight," he replied.

The crowd is in awe.

"Does this mean you're retiring? And If so, why? You are in your prime," said Bob.

"You see Bob, two days ago I received a letter from the United States military. They want to hire me as a combat drill instructor. I always wanted to serve my country and now I have the chance. I feel that there is no one left for me to fight. I beat the number one, two, and three top contenders of the world in good fashion. When I started fighting long ago, I loved this sport. It had it all. I mean, it had the punching and the kicking. Everyone appreciated the art, win lose or draw. Every fighter fought their heart out and even if they lost they still displayed good sportsmanship. Now fighters fight only for the money, they hold grudges and they're not even trained properly. Then they show no respect for those who beat them. The more I fight, the more I see all the crookedness in the business, and because of that, I lost the love for this sport. The most disappointing thing was Sunflower's gambling. I had inside word on what he was doing and knowing that made me just as guilty, so I did what I had to do. To clear it all up, I had him investigated because he was wrong. I wasn't afraid of him beating me in a title fight. That was real stupid of him to do. He was a childhood friend of mine. We took interest in this sport together. When I made it and he didn't, I let him be my sparring partner to get his foot in the door. I did all this for him and this is how he repays me? He was making money and he was going to be making more than he has ever made before fighting me. He lost his entire ranking for what? I really wanted to fight him. He thought that just because he was my sparring partner, he knew me well enough to beat me. He was and still is wrong. He was a dirty fighter, but I would have straightened him out in the ring. All the other fighters are good, Sunflower was better, but I am the best. Even if Sunflower makes a comeback after his five year prison stay, I wouldn't fight that crook."

A reporter yells from the crowd "You've got to fight Sunflower to be considered the best of all times."

J. T. stands up and says, "I am not going to put money in a convicted criminals pocket. He wouldn't last two rounds with me, anyway."

With that J. T. walked off the stage and tells them there will be no more questions.

CHAPTER 11

Two weeks passed.

There's a woman who is five-foot-six. She has on a modest dress suit. Her looks are somewhat plain, but trusting. Her name is Ms. Judy Brown, and she is the prison counselor. Ms. Brown is being led into the counseling room by a prison guard. She sits down in a chair at a table as the guard locks the door. Sitting across the table from her in shackles is the one they call Sunflower.

"Well, this is it, huh?" said Sunflower.

"Yes it is, and that is only because you finally decided to behave yourself," Ms. Brown says in reply. "Now it is time to begin. Name, age and how long have you been here?"

Sunflower smiles as he answers.

"My name is Todd Anthony Jones, but the Kick-Boxer Federation as well as the entire world calls me Sunflower."

"Why do they call you Sunflower, Todd?" she questions.

"The reason why is because of my mother. When I was young my mother grew sunflowers in our backyard and she called me her little sunflower. That and because of the fact that I was always seen eating sunflower seeds. To answer your other two questions, I'm 30 years old and I've been here five years too long."

"Todd, do you think that you are ready to enter society again?" she questions.

"Yes I am counselor, that is why they are letting me out on good behavior, isn't it?" he answers.

GARY O. MOORE

Ms. Brown stops writing on her note pad and looks up at Sunflower.

"Without this evaluation to secure your probation, you will find yourself serving the rest of your sentence. Now do you think you will ever return to prison other than to visit?" she says.

"I will never return to prison. I will die first. You can jot that down in your little note pad, Ms. Brown," he responds.

"I have one last question for you. What are your feelings about J. T. Lewis, a childhood friend and sparring partner who had you investigated for illegal business, which in turn wound you up with a ten-year prison stay?" she asked.

Sunflower just shook his head.

"I should have known then what he was all about. Well I had five long years to think about my old friend. I have only one thing to say about Mr. J. T. Lewis: May the **sun**shine on the **flower**s that will grow on his grave," he replied.

"With that attitude they need to make you serve the remainder of your sentence, and I should jot that down in my little note pad, Mr. Todd Jones," she says quickly.

Sunflower clears his throat.

"If that is it counselor I must be going. I have to prepare for my departure tomorrow. Guard I'm ready," yelled Sunflower.

Ms. Brown shakes her head as Sunflower leaves the room.

The guard tells Sunflower that he has a new fish he needs to break in before he leaves.

"He will be your roommate for your last night here, if you leave tomorrow. By the way Ms. Brown looked when I came in the room, you might be here longer than one night," says the guard.

"I'm out of here tomorrow man," Sunflower said as he walked into his cell. As the cell door slammed shut, Sunflower looks at this guy who is in the cell with him and asks him his name and what was his story.

60

A stern, but soft voice comes from the back of the cell which is big enough for two men to stand comfortably, but room enough for one man to lay in peace.

"My friends call me Chuck, and I think we should get something straight right here and now. I have never been in prison before, but I've seen movies about what goes on in here. If you think that I'm going to be your girlfriend..." said his new cellmate.

"Hold it right there, Charles," Sunflower said. "I'm not one of your friends, for you to be speaking to me like that. You don't even know me to be coming at me in all these ways. You really don't know who I am, do you?"

Chuck mutters that he kind of looks familiar. Then like a light bulb lighting up, he says, "I know who you are now. You're that kick-boxer who got ten years for gambling and tax evasion and some other stuff right?"

Sunflower smirks.

"That's sort of right Charles, but take heed to the words that I'm about to say to you. In here, others treat you the way you treat others. This is my last day in here. My parole board is tomorrow and I'm not going to risk losing it because I got into it with you. So check it out new fish, call me Sunflower, and again I ask you what is your story?"

"My story is simple. I'm innocent. I'm just waiting for my lawyer to get those missing pieces of evidence and then I'm out of here. If not, it would be life without parole for murder one. They seem to think that I killed my best friend or should I say my wife's boyfriend. He slipped up and told me about the affair after he had one to many beers. I thought he was telling another one of his bad jokes again, until he started crying. He had the nerve to tell me it was my fault, because I went out of town on business for two weeks. So being my best so-called friend he decided to comfort her while I was gone. I couldn't contain myself. I pushed him off of the stool he was sitting on and began beating him. I beat him until my hands were swollen with pain. Then I yelled for my wife to get in there and clean up her lover boy. Once she came in the room I left the house. I had to, or I would have started beating her to. When I was leaving all he kept saying was "I'm sorry." He was still alive when I left. I know I hurt him pretty bad, but I also know that I didn't kill him. If he received any deathblows it was from my wife not me. I really believe that she killed him, maybe by accident, or maybe on purpose. I don't know and I don't care. I just want to get out. That's my story," he said.

"Tell me Sunflower, what's the real deal behind you landing up in here?" he inquires.

"Well pull up a chair, Charles," Sunflower clears his throat and sits on the bed as he begins to recap his life.

"I was one of the fiercest kick-boxers out there until they dropped me out of the ranks for gambling, assault and robbery. I could never make the big money, and that was because J. T. who is the champion with all three belts wouldn't give me a title shot. Do you believe that man and me grew up together? We ate together, as well as spent the night at each other's house. We took up kick- boxing together at the age of 13 and even joined the military together at the age of 17. By the time we were 20 he made it and I didn't. From there he forgot all about me. He took me on as a sparring partner for a couple of years, and then he dropped me for someone else. I started making money on the side with my trainer. He had this gambling ring and I wanted in on it. I use to go the distance with people I should have knocked out and get disqualified every once and awhile. There's a lot involved with it. We were doing pretty well too, until I found out that he was holding back on a bunch of money that belonged to me. So one day before one of my fights, I confronted my trainer with my findings and he pushed me. He told me that I would get what he gives me and not a penny more. That's all I needed to hear. I put my skills to work on him. I took what was mine plus interest. I thought that was it, but the next week after a fight I was arrested. My trainer pressed charges against me for assault and robbery. He lied to the cops saying that he confronted me about gambling within the Kick boxing federation. That if he didn't go along, I was going to kill him. He also told the cops that when he said he wouldn't go along I started beating him while taking his money and jewels. Needless to say, I got ten years for the matter. They say good behavior, but I know the real reason why they are letting me out five years ahead of time. It's because they caught my ex-trainer doing his gambling thing with some of his other fighters, but they weren't going for it. They turned him in. He'll be here tomorrow from what I hear. One of my partners on the outside is supposed to pick me up. I hope he does what I told him to do."

"I here you talking the talk like you could have been the champ of the world," said Chuck. "The media always said it would have been a good fight between you and J. T. Lewis. Both of you would have gotten paid. What happened to the fight of the century?"

Sunflower stands up, goes to the cell door and says, "J. T. told the reporters that he would never give me a big pay day, because I was a dirty fighter and talked more in the ring than performed. That was about four years ago, but wait until I get out. I will beat all the top contenders and force him to give me that fight. I'll show him."

Chuck pats him on the back and says, "I don't know if you know, but Mr. Lewis retired from kickboxing and enlisted into the Air Force as a combat drill instructor just the other day. All the belts he held are now up for grabs. Vacant."

Chuck continued to tell Sunflower that J. T. told the press that he retired because the business is full of crooks and the federation doesn't seem to mind because they're not doing anything to stop it. He also said that there isn't any competition.

"Believe me when I tell you Chuck, I'll get my chance to fight and beat the undisputed chump in the ring or out. He can't run forever," Sunflower says as he smiles at Chuck.

CHAPTER 12

(On the other side of town.)

"Tracy you know that this is a rough area. Why are you so persistent on waiting for me outside?" asked J. T. while he opened the car door for her.

Tracy just smiles at him and gets in.

"Baby these people around here know who I am and whom I'm with," she says.

"That may be true but you don't know them," replied J. T. as he pulls off. "It's 9:35 at night. One night somebody is going to snatch you up and do awful things to you. Now promise me that from now on you will let me come up and get…"

"Shhhh," Tracy interrupted. "With you in the military we can get married now. I don't have to worry about you fighting anymore."

J.T. turns up the radio. On the radio was a sports broadcast that was saying, "For all you kick boxing fans, the wild man of kick boxing is back. Yes, Sunflower, whose birth name is Todd Jones, is up for parole tomorrow and plans on making a comeback. Word is that after Sunflower beats all the top contenders he would like to give J. T. Lewis a shot at the fight that never took place due to his conviction. If this fight does happen to take place it will be known as "The Brawl for all." J.T turns off the radio.

"J. T., why did you turn off the radio? It was about you!" asks Tracy.

He clears his throat and tells Tracy that Sunflower is a crook and a bum. He will never get a big payday from him.

"I have retired and there is nothing he can do to make me fight him," he says.

Fifteen minutes later they reach J.T.'s home where he opens the door and they go inside.

On the Westside of town a man is standing at the front door of a brownstone. A woman slowly opens the door.

"Hello Debra, do you remember me? I'm Sidekick, Sunflower's buddy," says the man.

Debra smirks as she answers him.

"How could I ever forget you? You were and probably still are Sunflower's flunky. You were the reason why we broke up. I couldn't take it anymore. You two were inseparable," said Debra. Debra I just need a ride to pick up Sunflower at noon over at the courthouse.

Sidekick smiles while he puts out his hand to Debra. She looks at him and tells him it's time for her to go to work. Besides, she is running late and she has got to go attend to her patients.

"That's right," he says. "You're suppose to be some big time nurse at the General hospital. I'll find another way, but you know I have to tell Sunflower how you rejected me with your ride." He then looks at his watch. It's 9:04am.

Meanwhile back in the cell, Sunflower is packing the last of his belongings. He can't believe that he is getting out of here today.

"Hey Chuck, make sure you keep to yourself in here. That is how you survive in the joint. If you get, well when you get out, look me up. I could always use another person in my corner," Sunflower says.

Chuck smiles and tells him that he will be ringside if, or rather when, he wins the belts. They shake hands and Sunflower calls for the guard to let him out. The guard comes and escorts

Sunflower to the judge's chamber to pick up his parole package. He has two hours of out-processing and one hour with his parole officer. Then his parole officer will give him a ride anywhere within the city limits. That was good for Sunflower, because he knew that Sidekick was unreliable with getting him a ride from the courthouse.

On the outside, Sidekick is still trying to find a ride to pick up Sunflower. He goes into a car rental agency. The lady behind the counter asks if she can help him, and proceeds to ask him how long he needs the car and what type of car he is looking to rent.

"I need something big enough for two people to ride in comfort," Sidekick answers. "I only need it for the day."

"O. K. sir," the lady says. "I will need your license and a major credit card."

"All right, lady, my license is suspended and I'll fill out this master card application. Is that good enough?" he says in an aggravated tone.

"I'm sorry sir we can't rent any cars to you today. Come back when you have the proper requirements and I will be more than happy to render you the car of your choice. Thank you for coming," she responds.

Sidekick turns around without saying a word and leaves, slamming the door behind him. He begins talking to himself, grumbling about how he needs to get a car by noon and it is 10:30 a.m. already. As he continues to hunt for a car, J. T. and Tracy are just waking up.

J. T. tells Tracy that he has three days until he has to report to duty, so he was going to make every minute count. He then takes a shower and cooks breakfast for her to eat in bed.

"That sounds nice sweetheart. I'll be here waiting for you," she says. She then turns on the television. It's now 11:27am and

Sidekick is still without a car or even a ride. Having finished breakfast in bed, Tracy gets up and tells J. T. that she would like to go to the zoo. They get ready to go.

Back in the parole officer's office, Sunflower has finished out-processing. As they get into the car, the parole officer asks Sunflower if he would like some lunch. Sunflower tells him if he is buying, he will eat. After driving a short while they pull up to a stoplight.

"Now that was a good fighter, a real champion," the parole officer said.

"Who?" Sunflower asked.

"J. T. Lewis. He and his lovely fiancée just drove by," he responds.

"Which way did they go, man? I have got some unfinished business with him," yells Sunflower.

The parole officer looks at Sunflower and tells him to calm down.

"I'm not following them. Besides, the diner is right here. What's your gripe with him anyway?" he asked.

As soon as he asked Sunflower that question, Sunflower went on and on about his plans to be the only man to beat J. T. in the ring. He talked while they ordered their food. He talked while they ate their food. He even followed the parole officer into the bathroom telling him how he can beat J. T. Lewis. He finally stopped talking when the parole officer dropped him off at Sidekick's apartment, but Sidekick wasn't there. He thanked the parole officer for the ride and told him that he will sit on the stoop until his friend returned. The parole officer told him to stay out of trouble or he will end up back in jail. Then he drove off.

Sunflower goes across the street and uses some of the money he got in jail and buys some sunflower seeds. While sitting on Sidekick's stoop spitting seed shells, he can't help but wonder where Sidekick is.

J. T. and Tracy arrive at the zoo and everybody who is into kickboxing recognizes him. A little crowd forms. The people are yelling out for an autograph. Every other person asks him if he is going to fight Sunflower before leaving for the military. He tells them all that he is finished fighting and now he is a military man. Then a voice rings out louder than the rest.

"Joining the military won't save you from Sunflower. You won't fight him because you are scared to be beaten," the voice yells.

"That's it. No more autographs," Tracy says as she turns to T.J. "Lets leave sweetheart. We can rent a movie and get some ice cream."

Watching movies was one of their past time pleasures. He would set the room up like a theater with surround sound and wide screen. Tracy would make some snacks for them to eat during the flick. While they are preparing to watch a movie, Sunflower was back on the stoop getting restless waiting for Sidekick to come home.

Just as Sunflower was getting up to leave along comes Sidekick. They were so happy to see one another that they forgot all that has happen today to them.

"What's up, Sunflower? Man, I have been trying all day to get a car to go pick you up and here you are chilling on my stoop," he says.

Sunflower tells him how he came to be on his stoop, but now was the time for him to fill Sunflower in on everything that has been going on in the world while he has been gone. After about an hour of getting filled in on the outside life, he tells Sidekick to show him where Debra was.

CHAPTER 13

After seeing Debra and talking to her, she gives him the keys to her car.

"You better be here to pick me up at 9:00 p.m. sharp," she said. "Now give me a kiss. Welcome home babe."

Sunflower obliges her by giving her a very long kiss. Then Sunflower and Sidekick jump in her car, blow the horn and drive off. Debra is still very much in love with Sunflower.

"Show me where J. T. lives now. I want to tell him personally how I feel about him dogging me out while I was locked up and about punking out with the serving the country thing," he says.

30 minutes later they arrive at J.T.'s home.

While sitting in the car they plot out how they can get him to fight Sunflower. Just as they are getting out of the car Do-little, an old friend and trainer for J.T., pulls up behind them in the driveway. The gate is closed. Do-Little got his name from J. T. because he seldom does things.

"What are ya'll doing here?" he says to Sunflower and Side-kick. "This is private property."

They laugh at him and Sunflower tells him to tell his boy that he is here for retribution. Do-little calls J. T. on the call box on the gate. A disturbed voice comes across. This had better be good. You are disturbing my movie. Before Do-little can say anything he is pushed down by Sunflower.

"Guess who? I'm back boy," Sunflower yells. Do-little gets off of the ground and tells J. T. it's o.k., he is going to go pop his trunk.

"You don't have to do that," J. T. says. "Not right now at least. I'll be right out."

Tracy asks him where he is going, especially since the movie is just getting good. He tells her he has to settle things with Sunflower, because he doesn't want him coming to his house like this. She tells him to be careful. J. T. gets to the gate and lets Do-little in and tells Sunflower that they are not welcome there.

"I would appreciate it if you would drop this fixation thing you have with fighting me," he yells.

"Fixation?" Sunflower yells. "That ain't the half of it. I need to fight you to show the world that it can be done. I'll fight you inside the ring or out side the ring. The choice is yours."

J. T. tells Sunflower to fight the current champion if he wants good recognition, but that isn't what Sunflower wants to hear. He knows he can beat them all but it won't matter. They will still think that he couldn't beat J.T. And he can't have that.

"There is nothing you can do to get me to come out of retirement or to even fight you. Now if you don't leave now, I will be forced to call the cops on you. I do know that you are a parolee," J.T. says.

Just then, Sidekick whispers something in Sunflower's ear and they get in the car. While they speed down the driveway and then down the street, everyone outside could hear Sunflower yelling, "I'm back, I'm back."

J. T. asks Do-little if he is all right. He says he is fine so they go inside. He tells Do-little that he can't stay long. He and Tracy are watching a movie. Do-little smiles and says, "I like movies!"

He was just kidding around. He just dropped by to say hello since he was on his side of town.

"Is everything all right?" Tracy asks.

"Yeah, Sunflower just wants me to fight him that's all. Don't worry though I told him that I was finished with fighting," J.T. responds.

Do-little says hello to Tracy and apologizes for interrupting the movie. He just stopped by to say hi.

"Give me a call tomorrow J. T. We'll play some basketball," he says.

Do-little leaves and J. T. starts the movie again. "Don't worry sweetheart nothing else will disturb us again, at least tonight," he says.

It's one hour before sunset and Do-little is washing his car. What he doesn't know is that Sunflower and his trustee Sidekick is looking at him through the bushes.

"Keep your voice down Sidekick. I don't want Do-little to hear us," Sunflower whispered. "We'll wait until he is not facing us. Then we'll throw this net over him and beat him down. Do you have the note for J. T.?"

"Yes I got it. Now lets go get him," Sidekick says eagerly.

"Calm down Sidekick. We'll go when I say go."

Across town, J. T. and Tracy are preparing to eat dinner. J. T. grins while he tells Tracy that they are going to listen to some Luther Vandross while they eat. Tracy perks up. J.T. knows what kind of mood that puts her in. He was hoping it would put her in that kind of mood. He was thinking of making a little love to her once their food settles. Tracy tells him that he had better eat a lot, because she was going to make him hungry again. They sit down at the dining room table and he begins to eat. Tracy stops him and tells him not to be hasty. The food hasn't been blessed yet. They lock pinkies because that's their way of expressing themselves as being one. Before J. T. starts the prayer, Tracy tells him to also pray for strength after dinner. They chuckle and then he blesses the food. While they are eating they discuss their wedding plans. It is very peaceful in that house. Both of them are feeling good about themselves as well as each other. They don't have a clue what is about to happen.

Meanwhile, back at Do-little's car, Sunflower and Sidekick are slowly creeping up behind him. He has his car radio up so loud he couldn't here anything even if he wanted to. Sunflower and Sidekick looks around one last time to see if anyone is looking. The coast is clear. At this point they throw the net over Do-little and say, "gotcha!" Do-little tries to get out, but the more he struggles the more he gets tangled. They start laughing at how he is trying to get out. Then they begin to beat him as if he stole something. They are kicking him in the ribs and punching him in the face. Do-little is wondering why they are beating him. Then he tells them that when he gets out of the net he was going to show them both something. Sunflower gives him the note and tells him to give it to J. T.

"Let's make him call J. T. I got his cell phone," says Sidekick.

"The only person I'm calling is the morgue after I take you two out," mumbled Do-little.

With all the commotion nobody saw the little boy who lives next-door walk up. The little boy saw them beating on Do-little. When they finally got Do-little to agree to call, the little boy tapped Sunflower on the shoulder and asked him what they were doing?

"I'm going to tell my father, the boy said."

"Grab him," Sunflower yells. While they were busy grabbing the boy, Do-little tries to escape. Realizing that he is too weak now, he begins to yell for help. Hearing him yell Sunflower jumps on his back and tightens the net around Do-little's neck. Then he slaps him on the back of his head and tells him that if he keeps it up they will hurt the boy.

"If you think we're joking why don't you give us a try? Make some more noise," said Sunflower.

Do-Little just gives Sunflower a mean stare.

"I didn't think so," said Sunflower as he patted Do-little on the head. Then Sidekick opens the trunk of Do-little's car and throws the boy in. The boy tries to get out. That's when Sidekick punches him in the face, knocking him out cold.

"Why did you do that, stupid dummy? All you had to do was tie him up and gag him," said Sunflower angrily.

"I lost my head for a second. He was trying to get out and making all that noise didn't help either. Besides, I didn't kill him. I just knocked him out for a while. When he wakes up we'll be long gone Sidekick responded, in a nervous voice."

Do-little picks up the phone and makes the call.

Meanwhile, back in the home of J. T. Lewis. Tracy tells him to light the candles. She goes into the other room to put on something more comfortable. He jumps up looking around for some matches. He finds some and begins lighting the candles. Just as he lights the last one, in comes Tracy looking as good as she wants to look. She came into the room walking to the music. It was driving J. T. wild. Just as their lips meet each other, the phone rings, rings, rings, and rings again. He tells her to ignore it. She tells him that her loving ain't going anywhere. He rushes to the phone and picks it up quick.

"This had better be good," J. T. says into the receiver of the phone. "Hello? Hello?"

He doesn't hear anyone. Just when he starts to hang up he hears a voice.

"Hey chump, are you ready to fight me yet? This is Sunflower," he says.

"How did you get my number?" J. T. asks.

"You can't answer a question with a question J. T. Now when are we going to get it on? I need to fight you man," he replies.

J. T. sighs and tells him that there is nothing he could do to get him to fight him.

"Oh yeah, I almost forgot," Sunflower says.

There is someone here who wants to say hello to you. J. T. hears a faint voice coming across the phone line...help me J. T."

"Is that you Do-little?" J. T. asks. "What's going on? Somebody say something!

Sunflower clears his throat.

"Now that I have your attention, calm down. Sidekick just put your buddy to sleep," he says.

"Sunflower, you bastard! I'm gonna get you," J. T. said.

"That's what I like to here," Sunflower says gingerly. "Once again it's on. You want me? Come and get me. I'll be parked right across the street from your buddies' place. Well, I must be going now. I have to call the paramedics. I wouldn't want Do-little to do anything stupid like die or something. I'll be waiting for you punk, so hurry up!" Then Sunflower laughs and hangs up the phone.

CHAPTER 14

J.T. tells Tracy that he has to go. She asks him who was calling him on the phone and what's going on. He asks her to do him a favor and check the hospital over by Do-little's place and see if he's in there, and explains to her that Sunflower and Sidekick jumped him.

"He sounded pretty bad, but I can't stand here and tell you everything right now. Just go over there and check it out. I got to go," he says.

"Wait a minute, honey. Where are you going?" Tracy asked.

"I'm going to get Sunflower. He's over at Brownsville Park."

"J. T., you need to call the cops! You don't need to get mixed up with that man outside of the ring. I heard that he has gang affiliations," she pleads.

J. T. interrupts her by telling her to do what he asks of her. He promises her he is going to be all right. She gives him a kiss goodbye and then closes the door behind him after he leaves. She looks through the curtain at him as he drives off. She wonders what she can do to help him without him knowing. Then she comes up with the idea of calling the cops and telling them that there is a drug deal going on in Brownsville Park. After she makes the call, she grabs her jacket and heads for the hospital.

J. T. drives quickly through the park looking for Sunflower. The place is crawling with cops. He looks across the field and sees Sunflower walking out of the other side of the park. He gets out of the car and starts running across the field towards Sunflower, when an officer stops him and asks if he has seen any suspicious activities going on in the park. J. T. tells him no. Then he asks the officer why did he ask that question and if there is something going on. The officer tells him that they got a call about a drug deal going on here, but they hadn't seen anything out of the ordinary.

Across the field, Sunflower mouths the words "I'll get you later sucker" to J. T. Seeing that made J. T. mad. He tried to walk away, but the officer asked him if he was o.k. He tells the officer he is fine, he just needs to catch up with a friend of his over there.

"Hey, I know who you are. You're J. T. Lewis! Can I have your autograph?" the officer asks.

J. T. looks across the field to see where Sunflower was, but he was gone.

"Sure, I'll sign an autograph for you, anything for a fan. What would you like me to write?" he asks.

Meanwhile, at the emergency room, Tracy is at the information counter. Tracy tells the information lady she is looking for Dewy Luttrell. The information lady is on the phone and has her back to Tracy. She slowly turns around.

"Can't you see that I'm on the phone?" she snaps.

"If you are talking business, then I'm sorry, but if you're not, you need to get off the phone and do your job," Tracy snaps back.

"Just know that I'm on the phone and if you want me to help you, you will wait," said the information lady. "What are you going to do disconnect the phone? You need my help I don't need yours." Then she chuckled and turned back around.

Tracy thought to herself, not a bad idea. Looking around she spots the outlet to the phone. She ducks down and pulls the phone cord out of the wall. Then she runs around the corner feeling good.

The hospital doors open and in comes Do-little on a gurney. Tracy is hysterical.

"Oh my god! Is he all right?" she yells.

One of the nurses put her arm around Tracy to calm her down. She asked Tracy if she knows whom the guy on the gurney is. She is hoping Tracy knows because they couldn't find any identification on him. Tracy shakes her head and the nurse tells her that they need her to fill out some paperwork for Do-little. She hands her the paper work and tells her to take them to the front desk once she has them completed.

When Tracy finished, she did as the nurse told her. Tracy goes up to the counter and says, "excuse me, I'm finished with the paper work." When the lady turns around, it wasn't the nurse. It was the rude information lady, and she was steaming mad at Tracy.

"It's you! You want a piece of me? Well it don't matter, I want a piece of you!" said the lady at the information counter.

"Miss frost are you being rude to the customers again?" the nurse inquired in the nick of time. "I want you to go change the bed spread in room 234.

"I'm sorry ma'am. We have been having trouble with Miss Frost lately. Please excuse her. I also want to thank you for the information on Mr. Luttrell. After cleaning him up, he isn't as bad as he looked. Once they get him in his room you can go and see him. He will have to stay over night, just for observation."

They both sit down in the waiting room. Before they can get into some deep conversation, J. T. comes running in. Tracy tells him that he is all right. She tells him to sit down. The nurse is going to tell us when we can go and see Do-little.

"What did Sunflower and Sidekick manage to do to him? Any broken bones?" he asks.

"I don't know sweetheart. I guess we'll see when we see him. All I know is that they have to keep him over night to make sure he's all right," she answers.

J. T. smiles as he sits down.

"You wouldn't happen to know why the police was at Brownsville Park at the very place I was going to meet Sunflower, would you?" he asks.

Tracy looks at J. T. with watery eyes.

"You should have seen what Do-little looked like when they brought him in here. They say it wasn't serious, but it looked like he was going to die. I'm glad I called the police. It's not like I told them what was up. I didn't know what you were going to do. You should have seen the look on your face. It frightened me. You better start thinking before you react. It can help you in the long run," she said.

"I suppose you're right," J. T. says. "I know that Sunflower is just trying to push me to fight. I just have to remain calm or he might get his wish. He got very close today."

The nurse comes out and tells J. T. and Tracy that Do-little is resting from the painkillers they gave him. She tells them they can come back in the morning to see him, and that he will need a ride home when he gets discharged at about noon. The nurse instructs them to make sure he takes it easy, because he has three broken ribs and they don't want them to puncture his lungs. The nurse tells him that besides some scraps and cuts and the broken ribs, he has two more badly bruised ribs and a concussion. Other than that he seems to be o.k.

Tracy tells J. T. to meet her at the ice-cream shop so they can unwind.

As J. T. puts his key into the car door, he hears a man yelling.

"It was you they were looking for!" says the man. J. T. turns around to see where it was coming from.

"Mr. Plowski, are you talking to me?" he inquires. "Yes I am," he responds.

"Well, what's going on? Why are you yelling at me?" Mr. Plowski is full of rage.

"I'll tell you why I am yelling at you. Just because I'm Mr. Lutrell's neighbor, it doesn't mean I have to be involved in his affairs. My son was locked in the trunk of your good buddy's car for over 45 minutes. He's all shaken up, and won't talk to the police about what happened to Mr. Luttrell or who did it. It took him two hours just to tell his mother that the guys involved said that they wanted you. What's going on Mr. Lewis? Tell me now or I go to the police," he says.

"O.k.," J. T. says. "I'll explain. They don't want to hurt your boy. They want me to fight again, but I'm retired. I don't know if you heard, but I'm leaving for the military in two days. They thought doing what they did to Do-little would get me to fight again. It's a long story, but that is it in a nutshell."

"Well, you just remember this Mr. Lewis. If this happens again I go to the police." Then Mr. Plowski turned around and stormed away.

J. T. gets in his car and drives off.

Ten minutes later he pulls up to the ice-cream parlor. Tracy asks him what took him so long. He explained what happened with Mr. Plowski. They get their sundaes and Tracy notices J. T. playing with his ice cream instead of eating it. She asks him what is wrong. He tells her he needs to be alone for a while to think about this situation because he really doesn't want to get her involved in this. He doesn't want to go to the police, but he isn't going to fight him. He says he is confused and need's a good night's sleep. So they leave the ice cream shop and head for home.

CHAPTER 15

Fifteen minutes later, they walk up to Tracy's apartment. He gives her a good night kiss and tells her that after he takes care of Do-little tomorrow, he will take her out to dinner and a movie of her choice. As J. T. walks down her stairs, he slips, but he doesn't fall. He looks down and sees that he slipped on pile of sunflower seed shells. Now he knows that Sunflower is following him. He gets in his car and drives off. Out from behind a bush step Sunflower and sidekick. They chuckle, and Sunflower tells Sidekick that Tracy will be the bait they need to get J. T. to sign a contract to fight. And they prepare themselves for the fight of the century.

The next day the phone rings and J. T. picks it up.

"Hello! Hey J. T. it's me Do-little. Are you coming to pick me up today?" he asks.

"Yeah, how you doing partner?" he asks.

"I've been better," Do-little says.

Do-little asks him if the doctor had told him about his broken bones. Then he tells him he is going to take care of the situation himself, despite the broken bones. He says when he gets better, he is going to shoot both of them.

"Just let me talk to them first," J. T. said.

"Yeah. Whatever," Do-little said. "Just be here at 1 p.m. and I'll tell every thing that happened the other day on the way home. That is if I can remember it all."

They both hang up their phone at the same time. J. T. yawns and gets out of bed.

On the other side of town, Sunflower and Sidekick get things together for their plan. They are both standing in an alley across the street from Tracy's apartment. Sunflower tells Sidekick that he needs to hold the contract. When Tracy comes outside they are going to grab her and tie her up. When J. T. comes he will tell him that if he doesn't sign the contract he won't see her again. They set up the video so they can show him proof that they have Tracy. It was time to put the plan to work. But he had to go see his parole officer first.

Meanwhile up in Tracy's apartment, she is making a phone call to J. T. The answering machine picks up so she leaves the message, hoping that he feels better than he did yesterday. She hangs up before J. T. could pick up the phone. He calls back and tells her that he will be by her place after he takes care of Do-little. He tells her to be ready at 3 p.m. and she says she will be waiting on her stoop.

At this time Sunflower is at his probation officer's office.

"So how are things going with you, Sunflower? Did you find a job yet or are you kickboxing again?" he inquires.

Sunflower smiles and tells him that he will be fighting real soon. They converse for a short while and then the probation officer says, "I'll order us some food. It'll be my treat." Sunflower has a shocked look on is face.

"How long is this session sir?" please!

"Didn't you read your paperwork when you were released from prison?" the parole office asks.

From the look on his face he could tell Sunflower hadn't read any of it.

"Well Sunflower, our sessions will be two hours long," said the officer. "Do you have something to do? It's only 1:45pm. We'll be out at 3:00pm."

"Can we cut this session short today, Sunflower asks? There is something I have to do!"

"I'm sorry Sunflower. I can't stop you from leaving, but if you do, it's back to prison for you. Now what would you like to eat?" he said.

On the other side of town J. T. runs into Do-little's room. He apologizes for being late, but he had a flat tire on his car.

"Wow, you got two black eyes," J. T. said.

"Shut up J. T. I could have taken both of them with my .45, but they threw a net over me when I had my back turned. I'll tell you about it when we get in the car, let's go. I'll check out while you get the car. I'll meet you out front," he says.

Five minutes later, J. T. pulls up in front of the hospital. He opens the car door and tells Do-little to tell him all the details. Do-little tries to get comfortable, but his ribs won't let him. As they drive off, Do-little begins to tell his story of the incident. A little later they arrive at Do-little's place. Before he gets out J. T. asks him if he remembered Mr. Plowski's son being out there. Do-little tells him they threw him in the trunk. Then J.T. told him how Mr. Plowski jumped all over him at the hospital.

J.T. drops Do-little off and heads over to get Tracy. He is already running late. He tells Do-little that she's nervous about him joining the military, but happy that they can now get married. He tells Do-little to go get some rest and take it easy for a while.

Meanwhile, Tracy is sitting on her stoop wondering what is taking J. T. so long to pick her up. So she calls Do-little. She figures he and J.T. are probably running their mouths. She gets up to go back in her apartment. Sidekick sees her going back in and thinks to himself that it is now or never. So he takes off towards Tracy. She sees him coming and runs inside. Before she can close her door, he sticks his foot inside.

"Sit down," Sidekick yells at her. "We are going to sit here and wait for Sunflower."

"Why are you doing this?" Tracy says to him.

"Shut up girl, before I gag you. I wish Sunflower would hurry up. This isn't the plan. I don't know what to do," he says nervously.

"Why don't you think for yourself," Tracy says. "You are going down for this. Why go down for Sunflower? He wouldn't go down for you, would he?"

At that point Sidekick pulls out a bag of sunflower seeds and begins to eat them. Tracy slaps them out of his hand and tells him not to ignore her. He grabs her by the hair and slaps her face. Tracy starts kicking him. Then he grabs her neck and starts to squeezing so hard that she passes out. When he let her go, she fell right through the glass coffee table. Now she is laying on the floor passed out and bleeding. He panics and runs outside. He runs around the corner right into Sunflower.

"Sidekick, what are you doing here? You're suppose to be keeping an eye on Tracy," he says.

"I panicked Sunflower. She's back in her apartment on the floor. I'm sorry, I lost my head," Sidekick said while whimpering.

"We got to get her out of there before J. T. gets here," Sunflower says. "Is she dead?"

"No," Sidekick said. But he's not really sure. They go back into her apartment and Sunflower decides to take her to the old abandon shack in Brownsville Park. Sidekick opens the door to see if the coast is clear, but it's not. Standing before him is one of Tracy neighbors inquiring about the racket that she heard not too long ago. Sidekick tells her that Tracy is drunk and they are taking her to Brownsville Park to meet J. T. He's trying not to be nervous, but he can't help it. The neighbor sees blood on his shirt. She plays it off and says o.k. Then she goes back to her apartment. The lady is looking through her door that she has slightly open. She sees them put Tracy in their car. As they pull off, J. T. pulls up. As he walks up to the stoop, Tracy's neighbor runs up to him and she is very hysterical. She tells him she thinks something is wrong with Tracy.

"Why do you think that," he asks?

"She tells him everything she saw as well as what Sidekick told her."

J. T. thanks Jackie and runs into Tracy apartment to call Do-little. When he gets there he sees the mess.

"I'm going to kill them both," he says. He gets Do-little on the phone and tells him to meet him Brownsville Park. Do-little asks why, and he tells him what happened. J. T. tells Jackie to call the cops in one hour, tell them what happened, and tell them to go to Brownsville Park.

Do-little is getting ready to go to the park. This is what I've been waiting for he says to himself. With his broken and bruised ribs Do-little gets dressed. Twenty minutes later he gets in his car and drives down the street yelling, "lets get ready to rumble!"

Sunflower tells Sidekick to watch Tracy. They succeed in getting her to the abandoned shack without anybody seeing them. He tells him not to do anything else stupid. Then Sunflower goes to get some ice for Tracy's face. Sidekick is trying to talk to Tracy, but she is still knocked out.

"I didn't mean to hurt you. I hope you can forgive me. I just panicked. I do that from time to time. The plan was for us to hold you until J. T. signs the contract to fight Sunflower. Then we were going to let you go," he says to her.

This is really all Sunflowers fault, he thinks to himself. Why does he have this obsession with fighting him? He goes over to the window and begins to look out of the window.

CHAPTER 16

J. T. is at the park now and he is slowly rolling around the park hoping he sees Tracy. He parks his car and goes over to some kids that are playing on a slide. He asks them if they have seen two guys and a lady that looked as if she was hurt. They tell him no, but the teenagers under the pavilion might have seen her. One of the boys at the pavilion recognizes J. T. as being one of the all-time greats in the kickboxing world. He asks for an autograph and J.T. obliges. J.T. asks if they have seen the two men with the lady anywhere around here. They tell him they haven't seen any adults out in the park today. J. T. gives the boy his autograph and leaves. As he walks away he notices this little girl playing in a sandbox. He walks over to the little girl and asks her if she is all right. The little girl is fine. She is just mad because the teenagers won't let her play with them.

"Don't be mad," J. T. says. "I'll buy you some ice cream and they will be jealous of you. What kind of ice cream do you want?"

"I can't take anything from you because you are a stranger," she said.

"That's very good," he responds. "Always listen to your parents. Never take anything from a stranger. I would talk with you more, but I have to find my friends."

"You mean the guys and lady I saw go back in the woods?" she said.

J. T. asks her where they went. She points to the left. She thinks they went back to that house that is off limits. J.T. runs to the abandon shack.

Sunflower gets to the store and he picks up a bag of ice and a pack of sunflower seeds. After paying for then he takes his time getting back, because he needs to think this whole situation out. He figures that by the time he gets back to the shack he will have a plan.

Back at the shack, Sidekick is starting to have ideas. He's standing over Tracy looking at her while she slowly gains conscience. He asks her if she knows what happened or who she is? Tracy shakes her head yes and tells him if he touches her again he'd better kill her.

"Don't worry baby, I'm not going to hurt you anymore. I'm gonna make sweet love to you baby. Now do you want to take your cloths off or should I?" he says.

"Leave me alone boy!" Tracy says as she tries to fight him off, but she is still too weak. He rips her cloths off and pulls his pants down to his ankles. Tracy lets out a scream, but it wasn't loud enough for anyone to hear. Sidekick slaps her face and tells her to shut up.

"You're gonna love this girl," he whispers as he begins to rape her. He's holding her by the throat so that she couldn't scream anymore. She starts crying, but that doesn't affect him at all. With each stroke he squeezes her throat harder and harder. He is so into it that he doesn't realize that Tracy is gasping for air. Sidekick starts to have an orgasm and he is still squeezing her throat even harder than before. In the midst of it all, he doesn't realize that he has taken the life of J. T's only love, Tracy.

J. T kicks the door open and he is mad. He sees Sidekick with his pants around his ankles. Then he sees Tracy's lifeless body on the floor. J. T. shakes his head.

"No, no, noooooo," he screams. "What have you done?"

Sidekick tries to run, but trips over his own pants and falls. J. T. kicks him in the corner.

"You better not move if you know what is good for you," J. T. said. He lifts Tracy's head and tries to revive her, but its no use, she's gone.

"Tracy please open your eyes," J.T. begs. J. T. takes his jacket off and covers Tracy. "Good-bye my love," J. T. says. Then he starts to cry. Sidekick thinking that this is his opportunity to ease out the door. He grabs the doorknob.

"Wait right there," J. T. yells. "It's time for you to die."

Sidekick takes off through the door and around the shack. J. T. times it perfectly and dives through the window landing on top of Sidekick.

"Get up!" J. T. says as he grabs him by the collar. "Tell me everything that happened."

Sidekick tells him everything that was supposed to happen and what ended up happening.

"It's all Sunflower's fault, J. T. honest," he says. He slaps his face and tells Sidekick that nobody made him rape and kill Tracy.

"None of this would have happened if you had fought Sunflower," Sidekick said. That really made J. T. mad.

"Prepare to die," J. T. says.

"I'm not going without a fight," Sidekick said. Then he pushed J. T. back and started running. He was trying to get to the open park where all the people were, but J. T. was right behind him. With a desperation leap, J. T. knocks him down. They wrestle around a little bit until J. T. pulls him up again just to knock him down once more. Sidekick gets to his knees and tries to beg for forgiveness. He tells him it's too late and to take his beating like a man. Sidekick slowly gets up. As soon as he gets to his feet J. T. gives him a roundhouse kick to the face. Sidekick's eyes rolled to the back of his head as he fell face first in a pile of leaves.

"Get up Sidekick," J. T. yells. But he did not move. He walks over to him and rolls him over. His face was busted open by a tree stump that was covered up by leaves. J. T. walks back to the shack to get Tracy.

Sunflower walks up and sees J. T.'s car and drops the bag of ice. I hope he didn't find them, he says to himself. He starts to run back to the shack. I'm running out of options here, he thinks. He starts to call out for Sidekick when all of a sudden he trips and falls. He looks down to see what he tripped over and it was the body of Sidekick.

"Oh man, look at you dude. Paybacks a mother huh? I'll take care of this partner," he says.

Before he leaves the body he takes off his shirt and covers the face.

"J. T. I'm coming for you," Sunflower yells.

In the shack J. T. is holding Tracy and is reminiscing of all the good times they have shared. He can't stop crying. J.T. kisses Tracy on the lips and says "rest in peace sweetheart, I will always love you." Then he picks her up and heads towards the door of the shack. All of the sudden he hears a crashing noise. J. T. turns to look and sees a big rock that was thrown through one of the windows.

"I know you're in there J. T. Come on out," Sunflower yells.

J. T. puts Tracy down and runs to the window. He doesn't see anyone. Just then Sunflower runs through the door, and dives at J. T. taking them both through the window hitting the ground pretty hard. They both get up slowly.

"What are you going to do now J. T., run away?" Sunflower says.

"No Sunflower not at all. Lets do it," he says.

Sunflower starts off with a straight right hand to the jaw of J. T., but he shakes it off and says, "is that all you got? Did prison make you soft like this or were you always soft?"

Sunflower smiles and says he's just warming up. And tells him how glad he is that they are finally fighting. Sunflower was fighting to prove that he is a better fighter than J. T., but on the other hand, J. T. is fighting to avenge the death of Tracy. Sunflower was getting the best of J. T.

"After I beat you, I think I'll take Tracy out and show her how a real champion swings," said Sunflower.

J. T. rushes him with a right hook. Sunflower hops back, right into foot range. J. T. dropkicks him onto his back. Sunflower is rolling around on the ground like he is really hurt. When J. T. walks up, Sunflower throws a handful of sunflower seeds into the face of J. T. Then he gets up, picks J. T. up, and throws him in a pile of lumber. J. T. is groggy from the fall, but he knows he has to get up. As he gets to his feet, Sunflower kicks him back down. As J. T. lays on the logs, Sunflower picks a log up over his head.

"Now you will know how Sidekick felt. What am I doing? I don't need a log. I got something better," he says as he pulls out a gun. He places it on J. T. nose.

"Before I shoot you, I want you to know that I am going to be the next champion of the world. Do you have any last words?" he says.

J. T. looks him in the eye.

"I don't have any thing to live for. Go ahead and shoot me. You will have to live with the fact that the only way you beat me was with a gun in the woods, not with your fighting skills in a ring," J.T. says.

"Shut up J. T.," Sunflower says. "You are the past, brother."

The gun goes off. J. T. closes his eyes just in time to feel the heavy blow to the chest. He gasps for air and opens his eyes to see Sunflower laying on him with a hole in the back. Do-Little is standing there with a 9mm.

"Am I glad to see you, Do-little," J. T. says. "You may be a little tardy, but not too late. When I heard the gun go off, I thought I was dead. I had given up all hope," he said.

"See, you always got on me about packing a gun, but look what got you out of this jam, not your kick boxing," he answers.

J. T. slowly gets up and tells him just because he's right this time doesn't make him right all the time. He asks him to call an ambulance, because Tracy is dead and he needs to go get her body out of the shack. J. T. weeps some more before carrying her out of the shack.

CHAPTER 17

Ten minutes later, Do-little tells J. T. that Detective Shaw would like his statement on the things that happened. The detective tells him that he can either go down to the precinct or they can do this over by his car.

"Look detective. I just lost my fiancée out here. You can at least give me a day or two to grieve her death before you start interrogating me," he asks.

"I'm sorry, but this is what we have to do to start the investigation," the detective responds.

So even though J. T. wasn't in the mood he told the detective every little detail. After about two weeks of going over all of the evidence, J. T. and Do-little were cleared of all charges.

(One month later)

J. T. takes a few days of leave from the military and goes to the grave site of Tracy. Her tombstone was made out of marble in the colors that they were going to use in their wedding. It stood at 5 feet even. Encased in the middle of the tombstone J. T. had their wedding rings.

He does the same thing every time he comes here. He prayed over the grave and then spoke to her, as if she was going to soon return. Now it was time for him to leave. He opens his car door and sees a note being held down by sunflower seeds. The note read: You better get to Do-little before I do!" He was perplexed because he thought Sunflower was dead.

Ten minutes later, J. T. pulls up to Do-little's house and sees the place crawling with cops. He runs up to one of them and asks what's going on. They tell him there was a house robbery and the owner was killed. The owner must have loved sunflower seeds, they told him. He had them in all of his pockets, said the officer.

"Hey, wait a minute. I know you. You're J. T. Lewis the fighter, right?" says one of the police officers.

J. T. ignores him. He is confused and knows he needs to go see the detective, the one that was there at the shack that night.

J. T. looks around and doesn't see him anywhere. So he jumps in his car and drives to his office. When he gets there he goes into the office to find Detective Shaw on the phone. J. T. walks up to the phone and hangs it up.

"Calm down J. T.," the detective said. "I know why you're here.

"Why didn't you tell me that he was still alive? It's bad enough he killed my fiancée, but now he killed my best friend," J.T. yells.

"Let me explain what happened. Sunflower was in critical condition for a while. The day he was due to be released, we went to the hospital to get him. Unfortunately his nurse just happened to be his girlfriend. She had been covering things up, making it look like he was sicker than he really was. One of the other nurses on shift told us that she saw them leave together. We just got a lead saying that there are two people who fit their description at the airport."

That's all J. T. had to hear. He shot out of there like a rocket, but not without Detective Shaw warning him to let the authorities handle Sunflower.

J. T. was heading for the airport. Sunflower's fixation on fighting him was too strong for him to up and leave. After fighting traffic, he finally arrives and parks his car in the loading and unloading zone. The parking attendant tells J.T. that he can't leave his car parked there because it will be towed at his expense. J. T. ignored him and ran inside where he searched ten minutes for Sunflower, but didn't find him. J. T. had the feeling that he might not get a chance to settle the score with Sunflower. He was so wrapped up in thought that he bumped into a lady knocking her bag that she was eating out of, out of her hand and onto the floor.

"I'm sorry, ma'am, let me pick those up for you," he said. But when he bent over to pick up her bag, he saw that they were sunflower seeds. He chuckled and told the lady that he would buy her some more.

"What a coincidence," says J. T. "You're eating sunflower seeds and I'm looking for someone who calls himself sunflower."

Then he slowly stands up and looks at the lady when she tells him that Sunflower was right.

"He said you would come looking for us and you did," she says. Before he could respond, he felt a sharp pain in his stomach in two different places—one after another. He grabbed his stomach and fell to the floor. He looked at his hands and saw that they were covered with blood.

"I got him baby," she says. "We can go now."

The nurse took off running. While she was running she threw the scalpel she use to stab J. T. in one of the trash cans along the way.

Meanwhile, an airport security guard is trying to see if J. T. is all right. J. T. tells him that he is fine, that he needs to go get that lady.

"I'll live, just stop her!" he yells.

The guard tells J. T. that everything is under control. Then he points down the corridor. J. T. looks and sees Sunflower and his girlfriend. They are both handcuffed with two cops walking them back up the corridor towards him. Detective Shaw walks up to J. T. and tells him it is all over now.

"If you weren't in such a rush, I would have told you that my people were here all ready to pick Sunflower and the nurse up. If you can make it outside, there's an ambulance out there for you," said the detective.

"Thanks, detective Shaw. I can make it," said J. T. As J. T. was getting into the ambulance, he saw Sunflower being put into the back of a police car. He yelled out to him.

"See what your fixation did to everybody? Was it worth it?" J.T. yells.

Sunflower tried to spit on him, but he missed.

"You better hope I die before I see you again J. T., because next time there will be no games. I'm just going to kill you."

Then the police officers pushed him into the back seat and they drove off.

One year later the trial was done and the sentence was passed to both Sunflower and his girlfriend, the nurse. She was serving twenty years for assault with the attempt to kill, and aiding and abetting a criminal. J. T. was doing well as a combat drill instructor for the military. This was his only way to keep his mind off of all that had happened. J. T. never returned to kick boxing.

"When they told me that you were back in here, I had to come and see for myself," said Ms. Brown to Sunflower.

"Counselor, this is all a mistake, but I'll tell you about it in our session," said Sunflower.

Ms. Brown looked at him and smiled.

"You're only going to be here for a couple of days while your paper work is being completed. Then you go to the penitentiary. You got life with hard labor buddy, I only council inmates with sentences of ten years or less. It will take God almighty to get you back out in the world again, and you can write that down. By the way, here's some sunflower seeds, enjoy."

Then Ms. Brown leaves the room laughing, and all Sunflower can do is hang his head. All of a sudden he jumps to his feet and yell, "I will return, no one can hold me down, I'm Sunflower. Write it down people. I will return".

The old man begins to say something else, but right at that time he is hit in the face by a wet towel.

"Are you talking about me, Sunflower says? If you are old man, you and your friend there are going to get your asses kicked," he says.

I intervene by telling Sunflower how good he looked fighting in the ring and that if he was not in prison he would be champion of the world. They say music, but I say stroking the ego, sooths the savage beast. Sunflower calmed down and began telling us about his new appeal that was taken place at Leavenworth and if his parole is granted he will be champion of the world. I knew that he would never get out, but I agreed and the old man and me walked away.

We walked back to my cell and found a note, it read that the warden wanted to meet me at 3 p.m. It's 2:45 p.m. now. I better hurry over to his office, I think to myself. The old man told me to find him after my meeting and tell him what the warden wanted.

I approached the door of the warden, which is guarded by two prison guards. I show the guards my note and they tell me to proceed in.

"I have good news for you Roland," the warden says. "God must really love you. After two convictions you're getting a final chance to make something good out of your life. Don't blow it. Even though you're older now, you still have that boyish look to get you by. Make your rank back and stay out of trouble, because your next strike takes you out of the military for good and you'll be in here for the rest of your life."

"When do I get out," I replied joyfully.

"You will have to go through an out processing evaluation," he said. I didn't mind that. I just hope the shrink gives me good walking papers when I leave. The warden hands me an envelope with the papers I need to give to the shrink and dismisses me. I ran as fast as I could to tell the old man, but as I came to his cell it was roped off.

"What happened here?" I asked one of the inmates

"The old man was arguing with that big dude over

there and the next thing I know he's flat on his back," said one guy.

CHAPTER 18

As I worked my way through the small crowd of people I see one-person hand cuffed. It's Sunflower, and he's going off screaming at the guards saying that he didn't touch him. It turns out that he was telling the truth. The old man had an aneurysm that put him in the hospital. I never saw the old man again after that day.

That night I thought of the stories the old man used to tell me and I had to laugh. I slept well that night because I was excited about getting out in a month. The next morning came, and I ate my food as fast as I could and headed to the counseling room.

I knocked on the door and the door opens. When I look inside I see the most beautiful woman I have ever seen. I sit down and she introduces her self to me as Miss Helen. I don't know if it's me or if it's from being locked up, but I am really feeling this shrink. I think I'm going to enjoy the next thirty days talking to her. I ask her if she minds me lying on her couch while I talked and she said she didn't mind. She wanted me to tell her my life story up to the point of walking through her door. It seemed like a lot, but if that's what she needs to know for me to be free again I was much obliged. Something came over me and I begin to tell my life story to her as if I was the old man. Normally I keep my stories short, but with her I couldn't shut up. I told her that my life before the military was no crystal stairs by any means, but I'm not from the ghetto either. I was born in Rochester New York. I'm the youngest of three boys. My family was not rich by any means, but my parents made sure that me as well as my two brothers had everything we needed to succeed in life. Growing up in Rochester was not hard. It was the 1980's, the time of the break dance and rap was in the beginning stages of taking over the airwaves. By the time I was 9, I knew that I wanted to be a football player. People laughed. It wasn't funny at the time, but it is now. See in 1989 when I graduated from high school I was 5'10, 140 pounds. You can only imaging how skinny I was at the age of 9. Unlike the other kids in my neighborhood in the 1980's my parents decided to become more involved in church, which means that my brothers and I were involved. We attended a Seventh Day Adventist church. One belief that I believed at the time set me back in what I thought was my dreams was number 4 of the 10 Commandments: "Remember the Sabbath day to keep it holy. Six days shalt thou labour, and do all thy work: But the seventh day is the Sabbath of the Lord thy God: in it thou shalt not do any work, thou, nor thy son, nor thy daughter, thy manservant, nor thy maidservant, nor thy cattle, nor thy stranger that is with in thy gates: For in six days the lord made heaven and earth, the sea and all that in them is, and rested the Sabbath day: wherefore the Lord blessed the Sabbath day, and hallowed it. Exodus 20: 8-11. This passage is taken out of the King James Version of the bible.

What that meant was on Saturday when everything is happening we were in church. We observed the Sabbath from sundown Friday to sundown Saturday. Between those times we couldn't play watch TV or do anything other than praise the Lord. I used to think it was so crazy. I would go out for a football team, make it and even be a starter. I would be at every practice through out the week, but by the weekend it was time for church. All the practices were Monday, Wednesday, and Thursday, but all the games were Friday night and Saturday morning. Needless to say I didn't play much. I did get to see Sunday football games on TV, but that didn't make up for playing Friday nights and Saturday mornings. I do have to admit I wasn't the only Seventh Day Adventist on the team and there were a few games they scheduled for us to play that were not on our Sabbath. I would cherish those games in memory forever. In my early teen years I was into martial arts. Those classes were Tuesday, Thursday, and of course Saturday. I excelled in martial arts as well as football, but just as football all the tournaments and testing for your next belt was on Saturday and they didn't make any exceptions. Needless to say it wasn't long before I quit going. My parents didn't seem to mind paying for me to participate on the days they allowed me to go, but what fun is it when everyone is getting their yellow, orange, green and I'm stuck on my white belt. So after I learned as much as I could I stopped going. That experience taught me that if you don't see yourself making it to the end of something learn what you can and know when to get out. Some people would say that you shouldn't be a quitter. It's never quitting when you are learning some thing in the process. In the mid 1980's things were changing in the streets of Rochester. A lot of the kids in Rochester, including myself, wanted to be like the kids from the city of New York. If you know anything about Rochester New York, you know that it is not one of the five Boroughs of New York City. My parents saw that I was heading in the wrong direction in my schoolwork as well as hanging in the streets all the time. So their solution was to send me to a private school in Pennsylvania. I spent my junior and senior year there. I had a ball there. I picked up more bad habits there than I did when I was home. Well at this point in my life I thought I wanted to be a dentist. My parents both worked at Kodak and use to get me summer jobs at Kodak. So when I graduated I worked my summer job and then went to college. I chose a college in Alabama. That's where my brother attended, so I followed suit.

College life was great. My roommate was studying to become an architect. He was talented. He drew out my dental office the way I dreamed of having it. That time will never come, because after my first class of biology I withdrew. Then I enter into the world of computers. My new major was computer science. The thing to study in computers back then was Pascal and copal. My freshman year was the best academically, and then it was all down hill. The next year I worked a summer job and bought me a used car and shared an apartment with a friend I went to that private school with in Pennsylvania. That's when the partying started. Girls every night and skipping classes. I missed so many classes I had to do my sophomore year of college all over again. One day I woke up and I was 22 in college repeating courses that you would need only one time to pass. I felt really bad about my situation because my parents weren't poor, but they weren't rich either. Their status put them right in the middle where I couldn't get financial aid. They were paying good money for my education and I wasn't passing any courses. I decided to take the last half of the year off to work for myself and pay my own way through college.

In order to get financial aid I had to wait a year without my parents claiming me on their taxes. That was a long year. I use to laugh at the people, who partied weekends and studied hard during the week, but now these same people who were freshmen with me were getting ready to graduate and I was a year and a half behind. I had one main girlfriend from my junior year of high school and much of my short college career, off and on. I say that because she was the type of female I knew I wanted to marry, but I wasn't ready to marry her yet. I wanted to see what else was out there and I wanted her to see also. I distracted her to the point of dropping out of college and going back to where she was from. She moved back to California and told me when

I get myself together to look her up. It didn't take long to out grow the youth of the college age, especially when you're not in college. I needed a change, so I packed up my Hyundai and moved to California. I worked hard at trying to get my girlfriend to marry me, but she wouldn't marry me while I was working at Little Caesars. One day I was walking by a group of recruiter offices of the Navy, Army, Marines, and the Air Force. I said to myself, it would be fun to join up and pretend to be somebody I'm not and see what kind of things I can do. It seemed as if I knew the traditional way things are suppose to go, but I tried to do things different and off the wall, just to see what would happen, whether I got into trouble or not. I didn't pick it up until my ex-wife brought to my attention that I do off the wall things so I can have a good story to tell later. So on this day I thought it would be funny to walk into the recruiter office and sign up for the reserves. The only choice I had to make was which branch would I pick? Well let me tell you, I don't swim. Who am I kidding I can't swim. With knowing that tad bit of information, the Navy, Marines and the Army was out of the question. There was only one choice for me and I made it. I then walked in and on one side of the office was the active duty side and on the other side was the reserve side. The reserve recruiter wasn't there, but the active duty recruiter was. He asked me if he could help me and I said no thanks and left. That went on for three days straight until the active duty recruiter offered me some lunch. He was good. He took me to the nearest Military installation and showed me around. It was like the military had their own city inside a city, which later I found out it was. I was hooked I mean you can live on the base and never leave and not miss a beat in life. After showing me that, I said forget the reserves where do I sign. I signed at twenty-one years of age. I didn't tell anyone that I joined the service. My mother didn't find out until I called her from boot camp and even then she didn't believe me until she heard the drill sergeant yelling at everyone to hurry up and get off of the phones. I told my girlfriend that I will adapt to the military way of life and I will come back for her. In two years I came back to ask her hand in marriage, and we were. After joining I realized that I was part of an elite team. We are known all over the world. Everyone has had some crossing with the military, good or bad. I found out shortly after I enlisted that being in the service is sort of like being a celebrity. Not the money by any means, but being known all over the world. It felt like I was famous. When people find out that you're a military person they give you credit which I already had badly of course, free food, and discounts, sometime big discounts. When I was in my uniform I was treated like a movie star. In some parts of the world it was crazy. While in uniform they would do everything for me except ask for my autograph. I treated my time in the military seriously while working, but when I wasn't working I acted as if I was in Hollywood. I took full advantage of being part of this elite team. When I look back at it all, I now know what got me sent here.

Miss Helen asked me what it was.

"The female species," I replied.

"What do you mean?" she said

"Well, I had what I felt was the perfect wife, but once I joined the military, after seeing all the different types of women, they blew my mind. It took a year before my wife joined me on the base. I was 5,000 miles away and couldn't wait to get married, but because of my love of women, I just wasn't ready. So, I thought that if I had sex with enough ladies before I got married I would get it out of my system."

Miss Helen cuts me off to tell me that after hearing me talk the last hour she can tell that my weakness for women would be the death of me.

"Tell me about your relationships. I don't want to hear about your ex-wife or the City-Wide insurance scam. That stuff is in your records, but what's not in the record is what I'm interested in," she said.

My mind is running a mile a minute. I'm looking in her eyes and it seems as if she's interested in me. It's all in my head, who am I fooling.

CHAPTER 19

"My first big relationship outside my marriage happened while I was in Technical school with a girl who was from the local town. The female had piercings all over her body and knew how to use everyone of them for the sensation of sex. I wrote this poem about our time together," I say, and then I begin to recite the poem:

Forbidden Fruit

It ails me so, that you're not in sight,
Weekend week out from midnight to sunlight.
When first arrived we came solo,
I met you and hated to let go.
You wore his ring and carried his name,
Sunshine, would you even remember my name?
For years with another sharing my soul,
you come along now I'm out of control.
Our heart beats in rhythm as if synchronized,
Your tongue ring has me totally hypnotized.
Over the days I'd hope we'd see,
Why we should remember you and me.
But should we remember, our bodies just met?
It was special; I know I'll never forget.
There's nothing that I won't do,
For the feelings I have our true, for you.
Just extend your hand and you will see,

security, how strong It'll be, for me.
After what was said, after what was done,
It could possibly be you + me = One.

"I met her when I had a month left in technical school so our time was brief, but we packed a lot of good times together. The most memorable lady was ten years older than me and she was outside my race. I almost didn't marry my wife because of her. I met her at my first duty base. I wrote a poem about her also. That's how I got over women before I got married. I would put it in a poem.

Where I Belong
I've always seen the other side when I was home,
It never appealed to me until I was alone.
Now I am there, and I can plainly see,
The other side where I am now is not for me.
It should have took family,
Couldn't see reality,
So I put it in a poem,
To know that home is where I belong.

My friend sat me down and he made me see,
That being on the other side doesn't mean that I'm free.
He told me I looked content in the new home that I found,
I told him I wasn't and I must go home now.
I got to go home now,
Even though I don't know how.
But if I can get a start,
I know I can follow my heart.
To know that home is where I belong,
Home, home, home is where I belong.

I've said this poem I must oblige,
I've always seen the other side.
Their tone I've probed, but can I condone,
This world of mine, as my home.
This light side of darkness appealing to some,
Alone again what's done is done.
Pleasure or shame, I'm content to see,
This light side of darkness is not for me.
I've got to go home now, a brand new start,
A step at a time, towards my heart.
Home is where the heart is at, I've finished my roam,
Thank you family and friends, I'm coming back home…..

"That was a very interesting poem Roland, but your time is up for today," she said.

"Before I go, miss Helen, I just have to say you are the most beautiful lady I can remember seeing in my life," I said, taking a chance.

"Thank you Roland. Are you planning on writing a poem about me?" she replied.

I smiled at her and turned toward the door. As the guard walks me back to my cell I tell the guard that I'm going to marry her someday. He laughed and told me to keep dreaming, and it was like a dream. Over the next 29 days miss Helen and I got real close. So close that she got transferred to the same base I went to. Before she got there she had to finish up few things at the prison. It took her three months, but we talked everyday. She said I knew how to talk to women and make them feel loved. That is why she fell for me. I'm really feeling like the man now. Because I was working off two strikes—I had to work as assistant Barracks manager. It was pretty cool. I wasn't going to get a place off base anyways until Helen came.

One of my added duties was called dorm monitor. I helped keep an eye on the Barracks when the dorm manager went home at night. The only reason why I took the job was because it meant I would have my own room, and it was either that or work in the sanitation department. It was three of us who were dorm monitors, my good friend Joseph, Sharon, and I. There were three floors in the dorm and we each had our own floor. We did a lot of things together. We used to go to clubs, movies, and even played computer games together. Sharon was pretty, but are relationship was strictly platonic.

One day Joseph told me that he was sending a girl to my room that liked me. The girl who was coming knew that I was getting married and didn't care. So I cleaned up my room and waited for her arrival. I picked up the phone to call Sharon, because I wanted her to check out this girl to make sure she was good enough for me. Before I dialed her number there was a knock on the door. I was shocked because it was Sharon. I told her that I was about to call her. Then I explained what Joseph was doing for me and told her to go find out what she looked liked. She smiled and told me that she was fair skin and had a model-like build.

"How do you know?" I asked.

"Well if you would take a step back, you will see that the female I've described to you is me!" she said.

"Get out of here Sharon! I would have never guessed," I said in amazement. I was very surprised that the girl Joseph was sending to my room was Sharon.

Sharon was a very attractive young lady. I would have never imagined that she would have a thing for me. Of course, if she knew my background she might not feel the same way. We talked to each other to see if we wanted to do this. It was mutual.

So we had an understanding that I was in a serious relationship with somebody who hadn't arrived yet, but we can have fun together until then. That didn't matter to her. She just wanted us to have sex and spend as much time together with each other as we could. I didn't complain. This is the fantasy of all men, whether you can get a man to admit it or not. The fun began and it went on for the full 3 months Helen wasn't there.

Then Joseph told me to be careful because it looked to him that Sharon was getting serious. I had to see for myself. So I called her to my room and discussed her feelings for me at this time and indeed it was true. She told me that she was in love with me and knew that I was in love with her. I didn't want to say anything to mess up what I thought was the perfect situation, so I nodded my head in approval and reminded her what was still going to happen in the near future. I knew that I was going to be with Helen any day now, and it wasn't going to be her that I will marry. I played along with her for a couple of more days. She kept telling me that she was going to take me away from my girlfriend. I would chuckle and tell her to try.

Time passed by and now it was time for me to go pick up Helen who was three states away. The night before I left Sharon, we stayed up all night. She was trying to convince me that I needed her and not Helen. Then we made love and she began to cry. The sun began to rise and it was time for me to load up the car. I kissed her on the forehead, whispered goodbye and left. That was the last time I saw the dorm. It was easier to leave than I thought. Maybe because she was asleep when I left. I figured we were hooked on each other, but time always seems to make you forget feelings, so I wasn't bothered. I didn't know how hooked she was until a year after Helen and I decided to get married. I thought we parted on good terms. I thought she had put it behind her like I did. I was wrong. What was I missing? It's not like we even saw each other anymore. She was still living in the dorm on the military installation while I was living in a house off the military installation. I kept in touch with Joseph and that was only because we worked together at the military hotel now.

Joseph told me that she lost a lot of weight because of stress and she felt that one day I would come back to her. I ask him to do me a favor. I gave him some money and asked him to take her out and show her a good time. I thought that getting her out would make her forget about me. Again I was wrong. He tried to take her out, but she would tell him that she is waiting for me. I felt bad for a minute, and then I remembered the fact that she knew what she was getting into from the beginning.

Well, some time has passed since that conversation with Joseph and then it happened. Our paths would cross at the commissary. I didn't flinch. I introduced my wife Helen to Sharon as just another friend of mine. It went well, so I thought. They both smiled and said hi to each other. Then my wife and I walked away. Sharon did look a little upset, but I knew she would get over me soon. My life as a married man is on its way.

I should have known something was up when they told me I was being moved to a different department to work. Shortly after switching jobs I receive orders to go to Korea for a short tour. A short tour consists of a 1-year stay overseas. The good thing about doing short tours is that you get to choose where you want to go for your next duty base. The bad thing about it is that you can't take your family with you. You have to go alone. A lot of military couples break up because of it. You have to have a strong relationship to stand that test of time. I had ten months before I had to leave. As soon as I got home I told my wife the bad news. We discussed the situation and then we started to plan for my departure. I couldn't believe it. I'm practically still a newlywed. My wife and I just had a newborn baby girl. I had the choice of sending my family to the next duty base or have them wait for me at the old duty base. My wife chose to wait for me to come back and then we would go to my next base together. That was fine by me because I know of people who sent their spouses ahead to their new base and they ran off with someone else. There was one guy who received a Dear John letter from his wife telling him not to worry about her, because she met someone else and wanted a divorce. He hung himself the day after reading the letter.

CHAPTER 20

About three months after receiving orders to Korea I get a call from Joseph. He tells me that he got Sharon pregnant and they are thinking about getting married. I was relieved that she had finally gotten over me. We talked for a while and then he had to get off the phone. For the next few months I haven't heard or seen Joseph. It was like he had just disappeared. It's getting close to the time for me to leave and I don't know where Joseph is. I wasn't worried about him I just wanted to say goodbye.

One morning my wife wakes me up and tells me to look outside to see who was moving across the street from us. When I looked, I had to do a double take. It was Joseph and Sharon moving in the house across the street from me. My heart dropped. We didn't acknowledge them living across the street from us. After a couple of weeks they decided to come over. My wife, to my surprise hit it off with Sharon. While they were talking I took Joseph in the other room and almost jumped down his throat.

"What were you thinking about when you picked the house across the street from me?" I said to him.

He just smiled and replied with, "Why are you concerned about it? You're leaving soon." I thought about it and he was right, but I had to stress the importance of keeping Sharon away from my wife. I had him promise to do so. We went back into the other room with the ladies. It was real awkward talking to Sharon at first, but she didn't seem to be bothered so I didn't let it bother me. We all had a few laughs and a few drinks. Before we knew it 4 hours passed us by. Everything was going to be fine, so I thought.

The day was upon us. It was time for me to leave. My wife and I were all but happy. I couldn't be mad at anyone but myself, because I knew once I signed the papers to join the military that this was going to happen one day. So we packed the car and headed for the airport. Before boarding the plane my wife and I made a promise to remain faithful to each other. We were dead set on not being like many other military couples that get divorced because of a remote tour. I kissed my wife and my daughter good-bye. I want you to be good while daddy is gone, I told her. Then I boarded the plane.

This plane ride was different than any plane ride I had ever taken. I was the only American on board. I flew on Korean Airlines. The plane was filled with Koreans and boy did they smell. I wasn't use to the smell of Kimchi. The smell was almost unbearable. It took us 18 hours to get to Korea. Before I left I was giving a little card with pictures of food, taxi, water, bathroom and the name and address of the base I was going to. If I got lost all I had to do was show a Korean the card and point to what I needed. There were more things on the card, but those were the main things that I needed. The flight stewardesses didn't speak English and all the meals on the plane were Korean dishes. I wasn't eating any of that. I was seated next to an old Korean lady who felt bad for me. She offered me an apple. I took it. After 18 hours on a flight you would have taken it too. Once we landed and were clear to get off of the plane, we went through customs. I really was looking forward to some fresh air. After customs I ran through the sliding doors thinking was going to get some fresh air. Boy was I wrong. I should have known better. I should have known that if the Koreans smelled that bad, Korea was going to smell worst!

This is a place that uses human feces to fertilize their crops. They had no indoor plumbing, just a hole in the ground with a bucket of water beside it for you to pour down the hole when you were finished doing your business. If you are fast enough you can run outside and see what you did in that hole flowing down the street in what they call benjoe ditches.

Now I'm thinking to myself, what did I get myself into? I went through customs with no problem. On the other side of the sliding glass I see a person holding a big sign with my name on it. It was my sponsor. I introduced myself as "G" and then we left the airport.

On the way to the base I tell him a little about myself. In return he does the same. Then he begins telling me about what I was going to be doing on my new job and what I could expect here in Korea. We finally reach the dorm for which I will be spending the next year of my life. It was pretty run down, but it was livable with indoor plumbing. Besides that, I had my own room. That night I took my time settling in my room. My job gave me two days to get over the jet lag. Before I went to sleep I called my wife to let her know that I made it there safely. Since I got there on a Wednesday night I had until Monday to roam about my new surroundings.

After I called my wife, I called a friend of mine that was there. I used to work with this guy at my old base. We made plans to go to some bars off base after he got off work Thursday. This had been a co-worker of mine for 2 years. He left to come to Korea 3 months before I did.

Thursday night came and that guy whose name is Barry took me around. He showed me the dos and the don'ts in Korea. We drank a lot of Korean liquor that night. The last thing I remember was taking a shot of Soju. Soju is liquor that is not regulated in Korea. I've been told that it is made with formaldehyde. You can drink it all night and never get drunk. Then there are some nights when you have one shot of it and it knocks you on your tail. That's the night I had. Next thing I know I'm being awakened by banging on my dorm room door. It was my sponsor telling that my boardwalk was going to be this Saturday.

A boardwalk is a gathering of the squadron for the new people who are coming and the old people who are leaving Korea. What it consists of is ten bars that the squadron goes to. They go to one bar every half-hour. If it is your boardwalk you have to have at least one drink in every bar you go to. Of course by the end of the night, you're either drunk out of your skull or you're dead. It was a lot of fun with a lot of drinking and dancing. I was drunk for two days after that one night.

The job I had in Korea was classified so I won't talk much about it. Let's just say that we had to have someone in the shop 24 hours a day, 7 days a week. When the weekend did come and if you didn't have to work, you got drunk.

Whether you were downtown or on base in your room, you were drinking some type of alcohol. That certainly was my routine while I was there. If you didn't drink before you got to Korea, you did by the time you left. My friend and I use to drink so much we couldn't remember what we did the night before. We had a ball. We didn't work together over there, so when the weekend came we spent a lot of time together. People use to think that we were gay, because we spent so much time together. That was ok for people to think that because that just helps us more to not cheat on our wives. All that came to an end when it was time for Barry to leave. I still had a few months to go. I wished Barry good luck in his future endeavors and then he left Korea. He was on his way back to his wife. He went back to the "world". That's what Americans call the states when they are in Korea. That was the last time I saw my good friend Barry.

Soon it would be time for me to leave also. Three months seemed like a long time with Barry gone. I didn't have anybody to hang with. I even stopped drinking for a while and started calling home more often. I kept in touch with my family, even more the last three months. My wife told me to hang in there, that it's almost all over. I did what I had to do, because that's all I could do.

Barry has been gone for two months. Things were more boring now than ever. Then that Saturday came again. It was time for my final boardwalk. Only this time I was an old head instead of a new head. It wasn't fun at all without Barry. I just went through the motions. Until, we got to one club and I saw this girl sitting alone in a corner.

This girl looked very pretty. She was too pretty to be alone in a club. I had to go tell her what I thought of her. We chatted for a while until it was time for me to go to the next bar. Her name was Alicia. She was good-looking, young, and on top of that she was American. I told her what we were doing—hopping for bar to bar—and she was interested and wanted to come. She told me that she was in Korea just for the weekend doing some shopping. I did all my shopping when I first got there. If you did know, Korea is known for selling and making anything you want for next to nothing. I had them making me caps, jackets, dress suits, shirts, sweat suits, and mink blankets. The funny thing about this girl is that she was stationed at the same base that I was stationed at before coming to Korea and we have never seen each other before tonight. The night seemed magical for us. Maybe it was from all the drinking, who knows? When it was time to go back to base, I asked her if she wanted to save some money, and of course she said yes. So I invited her to come stay the night with me since it was only going to be one night, and

I could use the company. We went to get her luggage from the hotel that she was in and went back to my room.

"Before anything happens in your room, I need to know one thing, and that is if you are married," she asked. "If anything happens tonight I don't want it to be with a married man. You didn't think that I was that drunk did you?" she chuckled.

I thought about my wife and daughter. I knew that it was only for one night and I would never see this girl again, but next week I was going home to my family. Surely I could hold on for one more week. So I answered her, "No I'm divorced, but I do have a daughter."

She planted one of the softest kisses on my lips that I have ever had. I open the door to temptation and the sin came rushing in. She wasn't married according to her; but then again she could be lying to me like I'm lying to her. She asked me about my wife and I told her that she had left me for another man. That must have gotten her hot, because she started to rub on my chest. I sat down on the bed where she soon joined me. I wasn't expecting company, but I had my black bulb on and some soft jazz was playing softly. The mood was set. I kept telling her that I missed my daughter and how wrong my wife was for running off on me like that. The more I talked the more aggressive she got. Then she told me to shut up and get naked. I knew that I was making a big mistake, but it didn't stop me from having sex with her. I had some Soju in the refrigerator so we drank some and and had some sex. After doing that for a few hours we fell asleep in each other arms.

CHAPTER 21

The next morning we took a shower together. She asked me if we could get together once I finish my tour in Korea.

"Of course we can sweetheart," I said. I had to keep playing the roll until she left. She got out of the shower before I did so I told her to open my blinds for me and let the sun shine in. While I'm still in the shower, I'm thinking of the stupid things I did last night, but I also was thinking of how much fun it was. I've done a lot of things I should have not done before, but adultery was not one of them. I shook it off and started to think of different ways I could get her out of my room quickly.

After drying myself off I came out of the bathroom, and noticed Alicia staring at a picture of my daughter. I'm always trying to make someone laugh, so me being funny, decided to introduce Alicia to the picture of my daughter. Before I could say my daughter's name, Alicia said it first. I was shocked.

"How did you know her name," I asked. I was very bewildered at this point. That's when everything came tumbling down. She was hot all of a sudden, and not in a sexy way either. She begins to yell at me. Then she started talking to herself. She was saying things like "how could I've been so stupid? I should have known when you told me your name."

I'm just standing there wondering what's going to happen next. She kept going on and on and then she told me that she baby-sit my daughter a few times. She even told me what my wife's name was. Alicia yelled at me.

"You fucking liar. You're still married," she said. Then she sat down on my bed shaking her head no.

GARY O. MOORE

"Roland do you know who introduced me to your wife?" she asked. I didn't know so of course I had to say no. Then she said a name to me that I thought I wouldn't hear again.

"Sharon my best friend, and she told me all about what you and her had before you got married, and what do I do? I sleep with the guy I tell her is no good and should be taught a lesson about relationships," she says.

Sharon told Alicia so much stuff about me that Alicia, not even knowing me, hated my guts. I sat next to her and told her the truth about Sharon, my wife, and me. I then proceeded to apologize for lying to her. After ten minutes of saying I'm sorry, she finally accepted my apology. She knew in the back of her mind that she didn't know me and I didn't force her to stay the night with me let alone have sex with me.

I was kind of scared, so I took her out to lunch and we went to the terminal for her to catch her plane. Before she boarded the plane, she told me that even if I had told her the truth, we still would have had sex. The only difference would have been that we would have had sex again instead of going to lunch before she left. I was shocked to hear that statement from her. I gave her a hug. While we were embraced in that hug, she told me that she wouldn't tell my wife what happened here, not for me but for her. She felt very bad having falling for the guy who she felt dogged her best friend out. I gave a sigh of relief as she walked up the steps to the plane.

I called home a couple of days after Alicia left and everything was everything as far as I could tell. She didn't tell my wife about our one night stand. I try to call Joseph to see what was up with Sharon and to tell him about Alicia, but their phone was disconnected.

Well the day is here and I packed my final suitcase. I called a cab, waited outside, and that was the last time I saw that dorm.

My cab will be here any moment to take me to the airport. I'm not flying Korean air this time. I'm flying United Airlines and it was a beautiful flight. Our household goods were already shipped along with our car, so my wife had to get ride for me to get back from the airport.

The first familiar face I see is my daughter. She runs up to me and jumps in my arms. I carry her to her mother, my wife. All three of us are standing in the middle of baggage claim hugging. My wife kisses me and tells me to hurry up because our ride is waiting for us outside. We get outside and my wife shows me where our ride is waiting. I put my luggage in the trunk. When I get inside the car my wife introduces me to her friend Alicia, the same Alicia from Korea. I almost swallowed my tongue. It was about 20 degrees outside, but I was 100 inside. I couldn't stop sweating. Apparently my wife still didn't know about my affair with Alicia. Alicia dropped us off at our house and told us that she will be back tomorrow night to take us back to the airport. That's when we were going to catch our flight to my next duty base.

My wife told me that she wanted to check out Sharon when we got to the next base. I found what she said to be weird, but then she informed me that Joseph started cheating on Sharon with her best friend. What was really tripped out was that the best friend was none other than Alicia. Now I am thinking to myself that Alicia is a bitch. Along with that, Joseph moved in with Alicia and filed for divorce, leaving Sharon pregnant with their second child. That made Sharon literally crazy. The military medically discharged her, sending her back home, which just happens to be where we are heading tomorrow night. Joseph has custody of their son.

The next night Alicia picks us up as planned, but she didn't come alone. Joseph was sitting in the front seat of the car. I just shook my head. No one in the car said much on the way to the airport, and before you knew it we were there. Before we boarded the plane, Joseph pulls me aside and tells me that he knows about the one night stand between Alicia and I. That's cool he says to me. But he was not the only one who knows though. Then he tells me that Sharon also knows and I should keep an eye out for her. She's a nut case now. She blames all her misfortunes on me, he said.

"On me?" I respond. "I haven't seen Sharon in nearly two years."

This was crazy, but I didn't let it bother me much. San Antonio is a big city. What are the odds of me running into her? Then I think of all the other series of coincidences. Then Joseph tells me that she gets her treatments from the hospital on the base, the same base where I'll be working. Now I'm worried. Joseph and I shook hands, wished each other good luck in the future, and that was the last time I saw Joseph and Alicia.

Well a couple of months go by and everything is going great in my life. Then it starts. I've managed to convince my wife that it will be best to leave Sharon alone to deal with her problems. So we never tried to look for her. I didn't know that Sharon had already found me. First my car gets keyed very badly. Then I get a flat tire. I knew it was Sharon once my car window was broken. All this happened to my car, but never my wife's car. I tried to get the police to help, but they keep telling that with out proof there is nothing that they can do. I can't believe all this could happen to my car on a military installation and no one saw it happening. If I didn't know better I would have thought everyone on this base was helping Sharon commit these acts.

One day my wife, daughter and I were leaving the hospital on base. We were happy because we just found out that we were going to have another baby. I should have known when we left the hospital that we might run into Sharon, and we did. I had already put my daughter in the back seat of the car and was opening the front door for my wife when all of a sudden out from behind a big bush, jumps Sharon. She looked like she hadn't bathed in weeks.

"You like what you see Roland?" she asks. "You did this to me! We were supposed to be married, not you and her. I guess Roland didn't tell you that the year before you married him, we were in love."

I stopped her right there by saying that we were only friends. If you fell in love with me that was your problem not mine. Helen stepped back and asked me if I ever fooled around with Sharon. What could I say but no! Then Sharon says, "I guess you didn't fool around with Alicia when she went to Korea either, huh?" That's when my wife slapped my face and said, "How could you? You made a promise to me, no more womanizing."

"How could I be so dumb to fall for you knowing your background?" she yelled.

"Let me explain sweetheart," I pleaded. It sounded like a cannon, and felt like a truck, and then I realized what it was, a bullet to my chest. As I fell down my Helen screamed. I remember looking at my daughter trying to get out of the car, but we had the child safety locks on the doors and she couldn't get out. I could hear her faint screams, "daddy please get up", but her cries were drowned out by Sharon yelling, "We will be together again, forever this time!" Then she shot herself in the head.

"Somebody help, my husband has just been shot!" my wife screamed.

Helen held me in her arms and cried out to God. Why, did this have to happen? Then she looked me in the eye with a look I have never seen on her face before and said, "Remember what I told you when you were in prison? A woman would be the death of you." After she said that she laid my head down and walked away.

The only thing I could say to her was I'm sorry and take good care of our child. As I lay there in a pool of my blood all over the ground, my life flashed before my eyes. I came to the realization that I thought I needed all those women I slept with to love me when all I needed to do was love one. If its God's will, He will give me a chance to make amends to all the women I messed over, but for now I'm getting tired. I think I'll get some rest while I wait for the paramedics. I'll just close my eyes for a while and keep my mind busy thinking of a poem for Helen.

Ode To Helen

Our quality time was emerged in mass,
To deny me now I don't want to surpass.
It ails me so that you're not in sight,
The sun is setting no more sunlight.
More than I if truth were told,
Your whispers of truth are never unsold.
You beg to differ what I can't explain,
I now realize my feelings and words are never the same.
There is nothing in this world that I wouldn't do,
For the feelings I have are eternally...

That was the last time Roland Booker saw Helen, his daughter, or anything else for that matter.

The End!!!

Made in the USA